THE IDENTITY
THIEF

THE IDENTITY THIEF

R. FRANKLIN JAMES

W🌐RLDWIDE

TORONTO • NEW YORK • LONDON
AMSTERDAM • PARIS • SYDNEY • HAMBURG
STOCKHOLM • ATHENS • TOKYO • MILAN
MADRID • WARSAW • BUDAPEST • AUCKLAND

For Dorothy Ann Franklin, who read *One Thousand and
One Arabian Nights* to an eight-year-old and started it all.

WORLDWIDE™

Recycling programs
for this product may
not exist in your area.

ISBN-13: 978-1-335-40544-9

The Identity Thief

First published in 2018 by Camel Press, an imprint of
Epicenter Press Inc. This edition published in 2021.

Copyright © 2018 by R. Franklin James

This edition published by arrangement with Harlequin Books S.A.

For questions and comments about the quality of this book,
please contact us at CustomerService@Harlequin.com.

Harlequin Enterprises ULC
22 Adelaide St. West, 40th Floor
Toronto, Ontario M5H 4E3, Canada
www.ReaderService.com

Printed in U.S.A.

ACKNOWLEDGMENTS

Hollis Morgan has traveled a long way since her induction into the Fallen Angels Book Club. I, too, have traveled a long way as her creator, but I could not have done it without assistance from the best critique group ever: Kathleen Asay, Cindy Sample, and Pat Foulk. They are great writers in their own right and I value their expertise and friendship.

Beta readers are critical to writing a compelling story. I must thank Susan Spann, Linda Townsdin, and Michele Drier, who put down their own manuscripts to read mine. There aren't enough thanks.

Then there are those supporters who are always there for me: Joyce Pope, Geri Nibbs, Vanessa Aquino, Barbara Lawrence, Carol Oliveira, and Patsy Baysmore. You guys rock!

Finally, I must acknowledge the outstanding professional support and wise counsel of my publishing team at Camel Press: Catherine Treadgold and Jennifer McCord. Forever and always, thank you.

ONE

HOLLIS WAS GOING to be late getting into the office.

She bent over to give John a light kiss on the forehead. His snoring stopped momentarily and then continued on. She smiled. She no longer complained of his snoring, or his corny jokes, or his yelling at the 49ers quarterback through the TV screen. He was home, and he was safe.

It had been almost seven months since he'd returned from a Homeland Security undercover assignment that left him at death's door. He'd spent a month in the hospital to recuperate from his burns and broken bones, and did yet another month of rehab. Finally, after a third month of departmental psychological assessments and debriefings, he was finally released for return to duty. Thank goodness it was desk duty.

She gave his sleeping figure one last look, then tiptoed down the stairs of their townhouse and out to the garage. The sky was just beginning to pale and the sun to rise as she merged onto the freeway.

DODSON, DODSON AND DOYLE, or Triple D, as its employees referred to it, was one of the oldest law firms in the Bay Area. It was small, well regarded, and fit her purposes perfectly.

As usual, Hollis was the first to the office. She turned on the firm's lobby lights, and quickly made her way to her office. She checked her calendar for the week. Other than today's lunch with Stephanie and Rena, it was back-to-back client meetings and preparation for a court hearing.

With single-minded determination, she took the top file off the stack and began making notations for Penny to follow.

When Hollis looked up again, Penny stood in her doorway. The middle-aged woman was a force to be reckoned with. Dealing with her no-nonsense personality was a small price to pay for availing of her sharp mind and analytical skills. As a paralegal, she was unsurpassed.

"You'll be late for your lunch if you're going by the courthouse first," Penny said, bringing in two more files.

Hollis glanced at the wall clock. "You're right." She stood and picked up her purse and briefcase. "Time got away from me."

"Well, it's the same time for everybody."

"Yes, thank you, Penny, for your…your keen observation."

AFTER JOHN, STEPHANIE ROSS and Rena Haddon were Hollis's best friends, and their regular lunches helped keep her grounded. Stephanie had come to her aid during a few life-threatening incidents, and Rena was a member of the Fallen Angels Book Club. A fellow book lover as well as a white-collar ex-con, Rena shared with Hollis the nightmare of having to slowly regain society's trust, and even more gradually their own self-respect.

Hollis was silent as Rena and Stephanie chatted on about a recent celebrity break-up. Her thoughts drifted to that period of time, not that many years ago, when she thought she would never get her footing back. When she doubted that her life would be anything but an up-hill battle just to break even.

Prison life had definitely soured her, but as she thought it through, it wasn't prison life that had cast her into a tail spin; it was her ex-husband's betrayal that made her lose confidence and trust. Back then she had built up such a thick shell around her that after almost nine years it had become a self-made prison. But cracks started to appear. She could thank Jeffrey Wallace, her parole agent, for the first chink. He'd believed in her unconditionally, and introduced her to the Fallen Angels Book Club.

She took a bite of salad.

The Fallen Angels Book Club had been the key to her emotional resurgence. They still met monthly and knew the members of their group would always have their backs. It was where she'd first met Rena.

She lifted her gaze and looked into two pairs of curious eyes.

"Hollis, where are you?" Rena asked gently. "You zoned out on us."

She felt a sheepish smile cross her face. "Sorry, I guess I did drift off. It's not that I don't think the exploits of Hollywood stars make for fascinating conversation, but I'd rather hear about *your* exploits. Stephanie, any interesting cases?"

Stephanie shook her head. "Oh, no, Hollis, we came here for a girls' lunch, not a serious work re-hash." She took a sip of her iced tea. "But now that you've asked, I do have this strange autopsy file—the body of a young man without any signs of trauma or physical ailment. He just died."

"You mean his heart just stopped beating?" Rena asked. Stephanie nodded.

"Well, didn't it have to stop beating for a reason?" Hollis said.

"Yes," Stephanie agreed. "That's why it's my puzzle for the week." She pushed her plate away. "But enough of him. What about you, Rena? Now that you're managing buyer for Barney's Pacific region, what's *your* challenge?"

Rena shook her finger. "Oh, don't think I didn't hear the tone of condescension in your voice, Stephanie. You think that you and Hollis have the corner on life's grittier issues, that my work world is fashion fluff. Well, I still have to deal with real people and real problems. Which brings to mind, Hollis, my other half, Mark, wants you to give him a call about a possible new client—she needs to probate a trust. And *that* reminds me, are you coming to the book club meeting Friday night? You haven't been to a meeting in months."

Hollis hesitated before answering.

"Hmm, I'll give him a call later on. It must be a good one. He usually doesn't come across routine matters." She paused. "I'll try to make the club meeting, but I promised John we'd have a quiet evening at home."

Stephanie and Rena exchanged looks.

Rena cleared her throat. "How's he doing since he's been back? You guys don't seem to socialize much anymore."

"Of course not. He needs to rest," Hollis snapped. She folded her napkin in a small square. "My God, he was almost killed; it's not easy for him to get back to normal."

"Not easy for him, or for you?" Stephanie averted her eyes to the remnants of her sandwich.

Hollis could feel her face flush with heat. "What are you two trying to imply?"

Rena tapped her mouth with her napkin. "We're not *implying*, honey, we are *telling* you that you appear to be taking on the role of mother tiger. A role, I might add, that must be terribly difficult for you to keep up. Where do you think you're compensating?"

"So now you guys are amateur psychologists?" Hollis said, failing to suppress a frown. "I don't know what you mean."

Stephanie reached across the table and placed her hand on Hollis's arm. "You're afraid of how you felt when you thought you'd lost John. You were vulnerable and exposed and you hated it, so now...now you're trying to keep him close so you never have to feel that way again." She squeezed her arm. "But it's not like you, so you're clinging to work and dumping your irritation on the rest of the world...and your friends."

"Because that's where you still have control," Rena added, putting her hand on Hollis's shoulder. "But you're still off balance because you're really angry with John, and you know that's even crazier."

Hollis looked from one to the other, and she could feel her eyes moisten. She gruffly shook off both their hands.

"Enough, I'm out of here." She stood and gathered her purse. "It's you two who are making me nuts... and...and angry. I think you're both way off base."

Hollis walked briskly to her car parked out front, but not before she caught the high-five exchange between her friends.

TWO

RETURNING TO HER OFFICE, Hollis looked at the messages Penny had left for her and punched a number into the phone.

"Mark, hey, how are you?" she said. "I'm sorry I didn't get right back to you. My caseload is really active now and you know what a glutton for punishment I can be."

Mark Haddon had started with Triple D not long after she had and was fired about a year after that. A co-worker had set him up for a speedy departure when he realized that Hollis and Mark were about to reveal the co-worker's illegal transactions. Mark had literally saved her life, and she'd introduced him to the love of his life, Rena.

They went way back, if not in years, then certainly in intensity of experience.

"No problem," he said. "Rena told me you were real busy." They chatted for a few minutes before Mark said, "I thought you preferred probate because you didn't have to deal with *live* people."

She chuckled. "I know, I know, but I always find myself trying to right some wrong and…and that's somewhat gratifying."

"Your clientele are quite, er, diverse. I can attest to that."

The both laughed, remembering.

"It's never boring," Hollis said and then she glanced at the time. "I can't talk long. What did you want to discuss?"

Mark cleared his throat. "I've got a client who needs your help. This is a very confidential matter; exposure could endanger her life."

"Okay, this sounds ominous. What's it all about?"

"Let's do drinks," he said, rustling papers. "I'll show you the file. We can meet at Petro's. Not the one downtown—the one closest to Alameda."

Hollis furrowed her brow at Mark's selection of the out-of-the-way restaurant. "All right, see you at four. I've got a meeting with Gordon first, and I don't want you to wait."

"Four o'clock," Mark agreed and hung up.

SHE NEEDN'T HAVE WORRIED. Her meeting with Gordon was typically a fifteen-minute conversation, expanded to thirty minutes as he fielded phone calls, texts, and emails. Gordon Barrett had been her supervising attorney for just over a year, during which he had surmised that her deductive skills were better served in the criminal, rather than in the probate courts she now served. Slightly above average height with a nice build and a full head of thick brown hair, Gordon had brown eyes that didn't gaze—they pierced. When focused on you, they felt more like X-ray machines than mere organs for vision. He excelled in bringing in, and winning, the firm's biggest criminal cases.

However, since he had no background in probate law and more importantly, no interest, he and Hollis got along fine.

"I've been looking at your billable hours," he said,

pointing to a sheet of paper. "You've really improved your record." He gave her a small smile. "I know you think I'm always after bigger numbers, but I wanted to tell you—"

His phone vibrated and he snatched it up to look at the screen.

"Hollis, I've got to take this," he said sheepishly. "Touch base with me later."

"Of course," she replied, managing not to laugh until she reached the hallway.

THE AFTERNOON WENT by quickly. After tackling a few last-minute files, she had to scramble to arrive on time for her meeting with Mark.

Petro's was a lively old-country Italian restaurant under the High Street Bridge on the way to Alameda, an island city in the East Bay. Alameda was only reachable through Oakland by car and boasted a top speed limit of twenty-five miles per hour. Upper-middle-class seventeenth- and eighteenth-century homes graced wide, tree-lined streets. It was a hidden jewel amid the hustle and bustle of the urban San Francisco Bay Area.

Her eyes quickly adjusted to the restaurant's dim lighting, and she spotted Mark's wave. After they exchanged hugs, she slid across from him into a maroon-leather booth.

"I haven't been here for years," she said, looking around at the half-filled room. She perused the menu. "I don't know why not, because I love their food."

Mark grinned. "It's too out of the way and probably easy to forget."

"Is that why you chose it for our meeting?"

He coughed. "I forgot how perceptive you can be. Yeah, that's one of the reasons."

He didn't expand on his comment, and a server came over to take their drink order.

"I'll have the Malbec," Hollis said to her. She turned to Mark, who was still considering his choices. "Let's order now—that way we can talk without interruption."

He nodded, and the server was quickly on her way.

"Okay." She furrowed her brow. "Now, tell me what's going on."

He took a sip of water. "I have a client—a friend—who is in the federal witness protection program. Lindsay blew the whistle on a money-laundering ring about three years ago. It wasn't big enough to make the news in California, but in Chicago, the United States v. Dorn Enterprises case was a big deal. In exchange for her testimony in open court, the feds gave her immunity, a new name, a new social security number, and enough money to start over two thousand miles away."

Hollis's eyes grew wide. "You are kidding me. This is like in the movies."

"I don't know about that," Mark said. "She hasn't had a peaceful day since, always looking over her shoulder. But…."

He stopped. The server delivered their drinks and assured them that their order was coming right up.

He waited until the server was out of hearing range and continued, "She did well for herself. First she opened up a small consignment store; then, when she could, she opened an antiques store. She's built a new life and has become quite wealthy." He took a sip from his drink.

"Why do I feel that it goes downhill from there?" Hollis murmured.

Mark twisted his glass on the napkin. "Because it does. For obvious reasons, after her relocation, she couldn't remain in touch with her family. She left behind her now sixty-seven-year-old mother, a career, and a host of friends. A short time ago, Lindsay was diagnosed with cancer and given a year to live. She beat it and the cancer went into remission, but still, it scared her and now she wants to get her estate settled in case it returns."

Again, he fell silent when the server brought their food. For several minutes, they each tucked into their dinners.

Finally he resumed his story. "She is resigned to her future. Her medical diagnosis was a wake-up call. Lindsay wants to spend the years she has left with her mother, but she's afraid that the Dorns will come after them. So, she's prepared to live and die alone."

"Weren't they able to get convictions?" Hollis said.

"They got convictions on most," Mark said. "But believe it or not, there are still four cases pending, and a lot of people are uneasy. Lindsay wants her mother to get access to her money and inherit her estate without drawing a lot of attention. I've convinced her that you are the one to handle the situation for her."

"I'd be glad to do it," she mused, already starting to strategize. "I just need to make sure that I don't leave a trail. Her mother will have to be cautious in her spending. Otherwise, they'll suspect she got access to Lindsay and her money. I'll meet with each of them separately and design a trust that addresses their needs." Hollis straightened in her seat. "When can I sit down with Lindsay?"

Mark gave her a nervous smile. "She's sitting in the next booth, waiting to meet you."

Hollis raised her eyebrows and turned around to face a woman looking to be in her mid-thirties. Mark waved her over.

"Lindsay Mercer, this is Hollis Morgan, the attorney I spoke to you about."

Mercer was medium height and build. Her thick, shoulder-length dark-brown hair complemented large brown eyes and a generous smile.

She reached out to shake Hollis's hand. Mark offered to call the server back to get her order.

"Mark, don't," Lindsay urged. "I'm not hungry and I am fine with water."

He looked from one to the other. "Well, Lindsay, why don't you tell Hollis in your own words what it is you want done." He stood. "Unfortunately, I have another meeting to attend, so I'm going to leave the two of you to discuss matters."

"Not a problem." Hollis smiled. Mark would owe her a favor. "We'll be fine."

Lindsay put her hand on his. "I'll call you tomorrow and we can schedule a time to get that other paperwork done."

"Sounds like a plan." He gathered up his briefcase and coat, and giving them both a nod, quickly left the restaurant.

The two women assessed each other openly. Hollis spoke first.

"I suppose you overheard Mark giving me a summary of your...situation. But I want to hear it from you.

We can do it now, or perhaps my office would be a better place to talk."

"Yes," Lindsay replied. "I think your office would be best. Mark spoke very highly of you. I wanted the chance to observe you, to make sure we're a good fit, and I think he was right."

Hollis found herself re-appraising her new client. In the full light, she was not as young as she initially appeared—more likely in her forties. Judging from her manner of speaking and tone, she was educated and from the Midwest.

"Good, I have some time tomorrow afternoon," Hollis offered.

Lindsay shook her head. "No, I have to prepare for an important customer who is coming in to view a china collection. Wait. Let me look at my calendar." She pulled out her cell phone and quickly scrolled through the screens. "What about Wednesday? Say, late morning, eleven o'clock."

Hollis didn't need to look at her schedule. She memorized the coming week every Monday morning to keep from being caught off-guard.

"That will work. Here's my card."

The young woman glanced at it before putting it in her purse. "Your office isn't far from my business. That's good. Here's my card." She stood and extended her hand. As they shook, she added, "Well, then, Ms. Morgan, I'll see you in your office on Wednesday."

The card read "Phoenix Antiques."

Hollis watched her hurry away. There was something not quite right about Ms. Mercer. She couldn't put her finger on why, but she felt uneasy.

THREE

As OFTEN AS POSSIBLE, Hollis tried to arrive early enough at the office to see the sun rise over the Berkeley hills and cast its first rays over the shimmering blue of the bay. It was her one superstition; that moment seemed to set the tone of her day.

Standing in front of her floor-to-ceiling windows the next morning, she watched as the lights on the Golden Gate Bridge and the new San Francisco Bay Bridge blinked off. She smiled; this would probably be the last sane moment she had that day.

"Don't get comfortable." Penny appeared in her doorway, holding a steaming cup of coffee. "Ed wants to see you in his office."

Entering the executive suite, Hollis looked warily from Ed Simmons to Gordon, who was sitting off to the side. Ed was the firm's managing partner, the high man on Triple D's totem pole. In his seventies now, he was one of the most brilliant and respected civil attorneys in the industry.

Something was up.

Gordon, looking quite smug, was seated in front of Ed's desk and next to an empty chair. The chair was obviously meant for her. She sat.

Ed peered at her over his glasses, his wiry white hair barely tamed by a gel-smoothed side part. "Hollis," he said, "Gordon seems to think you're developing quite a knack for tackling the penal code. If you had the opportunity to bring along another attorney to bolster your probate practice, would you consider shifting your focus to criminal law?"

"He's convinced that I should expand my knowledge base," Hollis said grudgingly. "But, yes, I'm willing to give it a try."

Gordon grinned. "Now, Hollis, you know as well as I do that anyone who can dig up as many deviants, bodies, and killers as you can simply by preparing administrative wills and trusts is wasted on probate law. Think of the billables." Gordon raised his eyebrows. "You've got the inquiring mind of a true criminal attorney."

She raised her hand.

"All right, no need for the hard sell. I already told you that I'd give it a shot," she said. "I'm just not as sure as you that I'd be good at it. Besides, I like probate law, and I'm the only one who can cover the firm's trust clients."

Ed clasped his hands on top of his desk. "I think a lot of you, Hollis, and I just wanted to make sure you were comfortable branching out. I'm going to put some feelers out for a viable candidate who can help carry your probate load. Criminal law will be a completely different venue for you, but I think you'll excel at it."

Back in her office, she wondered what she was being dragged into. Though not yet. For the next few hours, she was occupied returning phone calls and reviewing emails.

Her intercom rang.

"Gordon wants to see you in the small conference room," Eleanor, the new receptionist, said in her singsong voice. The sister-in-law of one of the partners, she had replaced their long-time receptionist, Tiffany, about three months earlier.

Tiffany was sorely missed.

Hollis grabbed a notepad and walked down the hallway to the windowless conference room. Gordon, who'd been tapping out a text message, looked up.

"Come on in, Hollis," he said. "You heard it straight from Ed. He's going to get you some help. I'm a little pressed for time right now; I've got a closing statement to write." He lifted a file from the table and pushed it across to her. "I'm recommending that you take this criminal case on your own." He tapped the folder as if for emphasis. "Before you...."

His phone vibrated against the walnut table top and he grabbed it.

He glanced at the screen. "I've got to take this."

Hollis smiled and shook her head. She was used to Gordon's constant phone interruptions.

For once, he ended the call quickly.

"Sorry," he said. "Anyway, to cut to the chase, we want you to take on this new client. This is a good criminal case to get you started. Nobody was killed, poisoned, or bludgeoned to death. Nothing like you've come across with your probate clients."

Hollis opened the file. "Very funny."

Ed stuck his head in the doorway. "I heard that, but he's right, Hollis. Based on your case history, it would be safer for you to take on a criminal matter." He chuckled. "And I've already started looking for an associate attorney to work with you on your probate cases. As soon as I get a viable candidate, I'll let you know."

Hollis protested, "Ed, an associate can't—"

"I didn't say you'd abandon your caseload. Your

probate clients are still going to need your oversight. I'm looking for someone with a solid work background and substantial recommendations." Ed waved a dismissive hand. "So, for now, why don't we give this reassignment a try and see if things go smoothly?" He glanced at his watch. "I've got to catch a flight for a meeting with Senator Clark." He patted Hollis on the shoulder. "Gordon, stay off the phone long enough to give her a decent briefing."

He left, and she turned to face Gordon.

Without looking at her, and texting with one hand, he muttered, "Let's go to my office."

Still tapping his phone screen, he led her down the hallway.

"Well?" she said, taking the chair in front of his desk.

He looked up and caught her gaze. "You know, Hollis, you're going to remember this as the day that changed your career." He placed his phone on the desk.

Hollis smirked and patted the file in front of her. "Let me guess: you're giving me a case you wouldn't touch with a ten-foot pole."

Gordon laughed. "Close." He opened his notepad. "But it's not what you think. Justin Eastland is a young man with reality issues. His father is my landscaper and a good one. I've only met young Justin once, yesterday, and he…."

His cell phone vibrated and slid a couple of inches on the desk. Hollis stifled a grin as Gordon sneaked a glance at the screen. He caught Hollis's look, and with a grim expression, pushed the phone away.

"As I was about to say, Eastland has problems living in our world and the one he's made up in his head. I think you should consider having him evaluated by a psychologist to see if he's a psychopathic liar. It might help his case. From the initial meeting I had with him, I don't think he's capable of telling the truth."

Hollis raised her eyebrows. She was familiar with the ability to lie. She considered herself an expert liar, and more importantly, an expert in spotting liars. As a child she'd developed the trait—one her family didn't always appreciate.

"What did he do?" she asked with interest.

"Identity theft."

Gordon got up from the table to fetch two bottles of water from the refrigerator in his credenza. Hollis knew enough about his pausing for dramatic effect to remain silent. She was rewarded when he returned to his chair and gave her an appreciative smile.

"Evidently," he continued, "according to the police anyway, Eastland was stopped for a routine traffic violation. In his backseat was a gym bag that had spilled out numerous credit cards, four passports, and a set of professional burglar tools."

At this, Hollis re-opened the file and scanned the arrest sheet.

Gordon shook his head. "According to his sheet, if he hadn't tried to avoid police discovery by trying to put the bag on the car floor, it wouldn't have tipped over."

"It didn't help that he had two driver's licenses, either," Hollis said, pointing to a sentence, "neither of which belonged to him."

Gordon shook his head. "He's not the sharpest pencil in the box." He glanced down at his phone, which had just sent out a reminder *ding*. He spoke rapidly. "Anyway, I want you to read through the file and make an appointment to see Eastland. They're holding him at the county jail until the arraignment."

There was the sound of a series of soft bells. Twitching, he grabbed his phone like an alcoholic reaching for a drink.

"Yeah, uh-huh, uh-huh, I'll get right back to you." Clicking off, he gave Hollis a sheepish look. "I've got to follow up on this. Let's talk later this afternoon. I've got something else I want to speak with you about."

Hollis stood. "Not a problem. I'll go to the jail and have a conversation with Eastland." She walked to the door.

"Yeah, yeah, sounds good." Gordon was already punching numbers into his phone.

THE JAIL WAS located in the hillside just west of Interstate 580 to the rear of two busy suburban areas in Russell County. As Hollis descended from the top of the hill separating Livermore Valley from the East Bay, her eyes sought a distant building with a guard tower and an entry gate. Surrounded by a rectangular wall of cyclone fencing, it was settled in the middle of the basin like a boulder in a pond. Multiple layers of barbed wire, set off a few feet outside the wall, enclosed the structure like shrink wrap. The jail, isolated in a field of rolling green meadows and copses of trees, gave the impression of peace and menace at the same time.

Gordon had told her he'd been there so often visiting clients that the guards had teased him with his name printed on a mock "Reserved For" sign, assigned to a distant parking space.

Hollis had only been there once before, but it was to accompany a client visiting his son who had just received a major inheritance from his grandmother. They'd met in a small interview room. The twelve-month stint in the county jail, accompanied by the generous gift of money, turned out to be just the incentive the young man needed to turn his life around. He now had a practice as a life coach.

The entry's metal detector opened to the jail's public area. The swirl of shades of gray tint in the concrete floors suited the cold sterility of the space. Muted pale-blue walls and high-placed windows added to the sense of isolation and bleakness. A counter the width of the room stood at one end, supported by a wall of doubled Plexiglas. It faced a roomful of chairs arranged theater-style. A small round table off to the side was meant to serve those unfortunate enough to have to bring small children. She turned her eyes away from the disheartening sight of faded storybooks and mismatched building blocks.

Hollis walked up to the counter's sole occupant, gave the woman her client's name, and handed over her identification through the small opening in the Plexiglas.

The middle-aged woman at the reception desk appeared to have been squeezed into her deputy uniform. The buttons on her shirt screamed escape, and Hollis wondered vaguely what would happen if she had to sneeze. The woman looked at her picture and then peered at her.

"Take a seat," the receptionist said. "Another deputy will be out to escort you to an interview room so you can see your client in private."

With a nod, Hollis turned to face the half-filled waiting room of visitors occupied with their own thoughts. Most were professionals, probably lawyers, since regular visiting hours were over. Sitting in the front row, she took out her cellphone; she'd only gone through a few emails when her name was called from a door opposite.

Hollis walked briskly, trying to keep up with the tall thin deputy sheriff who led the way. "This is my first time here to visit a client," she said. "Any procedure or whatever I should know about?"

He looked down at her with a searching glance then smiled. "Nah, your guy is okay. You'll be all right."

Hollis shook her head. "No, I don't mean from danger. I'm not afraid. Are there any rules I need to follow?"

"Oh, sorry," he said. "No, it's pretty much your show. Just tap on the door when you're through. The sheriff is generous with visitor time for first offenders and their attorneys."

He opened a beige door with a small window.

"This is your stop. I'll be back with Eastland in a few minutes."

Hollis walked into the small room.

Just like in the movies. There was a metal table with two chairs on either side. Light came from two small windows about a foot from the ceiling, and overhead fluorescent light fixtures were centered in the room. She'd just taken out her notebook and pen when the door opened and her client was escorted in.

Justin Eastland didn't look old enough to drink. From his file, Hollis knew he was twenty-four and a native Californian. He was of medium build, with light brown hair and hazel eyes. Raised in a modest San Lorenzo home by both parents, he was a high school graduate with average grades. Actually, there was nothing outstanding about him except that he appeared to be a professional hacker.

She held out her hand.

"I'm Hollis Morgan, Justin. If you agree, I'm going to be your defense attorney."

He shook her hand firmly and gave her a shy smile.

"My mom told me she'd hired a lawyer, but I guess I was expecting a dude—your name and everything, no offense."

Hollis smiled as they both sat down. "None taken. Our firm has a pretty diverse group of attorneys. I have to let you know that I've been in practice for a few years, in Probate not Criminal Law, but after reviewing your case, I feel comfortable that I can help you."

Eastland folded his hands on the table and leaned forward. "How does it look?"

"To be honest, not good." Hollis observed him. "Why don't you tell me what happened?"

He squirmed in his seat. "Okay, well, I was driving through this intersection. The light had just barely turned red when I saw the cop car's lights—"

"No, not how you got caught," Hollis said. "Tell me about the gym bag."

He averted his eyes. "Oh, that. Why don't we just say that I got in with a bad crowd. They threatened me and forced me to steal people's IDs."

"Why don't we just say the truth?" She smiled. "What crowd? What did they have on you?"

He blinked several times. "These guys I know from work. They work for the Mafia. Anyway, I borrowed money from one of them, and I couldn't pay it back, so they forced me to do a job."

He was lying.

Hollis leaned back in her chair and let the silence hang between them. Eastland shifted, as if to get comfortable. He finally looked her in the eyes.

He frowned. "Why are you looking at me like that? Don't you believe me?"

"No, I don't," Hollis said. "Want to try again?"

He ran his fingers through his hair. "All right, you got me. I was covering up for a friend." Eastland rubbed the back of his neck. "I didn't think you'd believe I'd be so dumb as to trust someone who told me to hold their bag for them."

She sighed and shook her head.

"It's true," he insisted. "This friend of mine…well, he's not really a friend, more like a good customer I was trying to help out. Well, anyway he asked me to hold onto his sports bag until he came back from his ex-wife's house. If she knew he had money for a gym membership, she'd haul his butt back to court for—"

"Really, Justin?" Hollis broke in. "That's the best you can do?" She leaned across the desk. "I work for you. There is nothing you tell me that I can tell anyone else. There is nothing so bad that I would walk away and leave you without representation. That said, I know when you're lying—call it a gift of mine. I have neither the time nor the inclination to listen to your wild tales. Now, let's start over. Yes, or no, did you steal the IDs?"

"But you don't understand—"

"Yes or no."

He got up, walked in a little circle, then sat back down.

"Yes, but—"

Hollis shook her head and scribbled a note. "Good, now *that* I believe. We have a starting point. The police file shows that there were numerous victims. You tell me how many."

He clasped his hands and scowled. "That's what I wanted to tell you. I only snagged the gym bag in Putnam Park. I'm just a hacker, not an identity thief. I work with computers, not the real deal."

She frowned. "I'm sorry, I'm confused. Aren't you stealing identities when you hack computers?"

"Yeah, but you don't see the people. You don't have their *stuff*," he insisted. "I didn't know what was in that bag."

Hollis couldn't hide her disbelief that Eastland had never looked in the bag he'd snatched. He went on to say that it had been late, and he'd been looking down and texting a message when he caught sight of a black Nike bag under a hedge near an apartment building. He didn't see anybody around, so he took it.

Hollis furrowed her forehead. "You know that raises a few questions. First, do you usually take things that don't belong to you, and second, how did you see the black Nike bag in the dark?" She gave him a hard look. "I still don't think you're telling me the whole truth."

Eastland looked over his shoulder as if expecting to see someone listening in. "Yeah, you've probably seen my record. I've been convicted once before for burglary, but I was a juvenile." He shrugged. "I couldn't get it together after high school, so I was caught breaking into this old couple's house in San Leandro. I didn't know their son who was visiting was a cop." He shook his head. "My mom used to say, if it wasn't for bad luck, I wouldn't have any luck at all."

"Excuse me if I don't commiserate with you," Hollis snapped. "How did you really get your hands on the Nike bag?"

He held up his hands. "Now, this is the truth, I swear." He scratched his nose. "It's true I saw the Nike bag in the bushes, but…but I saw a dude leave it there."

"So, let me understand…you can identify the real identity thief?"

"Well, no, because it was dark like I said, and I could only see his shape. But I did see him drop the bag."

Hollis looked him in the eyes and scribbled more notes. "Okay, let's move on. Did you open the bag?"

Eastland shook his head. "Nah, I just snatched it and ran to my car. And I was driving back to my place when the cops stopped me, and everything fell out of the bag."

"So, until the police stopped you, you had no idea what you had picked up?"

He held up his hand. "I swear."

He was lying.

"How did the stuff slip out on the floor of the backseat if you hadn't left it open?" Hollis leaned back in her chair. "I find it really hard to bel—"

She was interrupted by a loud knock. Two uniformed officers and a deputy sheriff entered the room, followed by a suited man holding out a badge.

"Excuse me, Counselor," the man with the badge said. "I'm Detective Cook with the county sheriff. We're here for your client." He nodded toward the young man. "Justin Eastland," he said, "we are arresting you for the murder of Marguerite Fields." He turned to one of the officers. "Read him his rights." To Eastland, he said, "Please follow us."

For a moment, Hollis stood transfixed as the officer droned on with the required wording, and then she spoke. "As his attorney, I can tell you that he is not talking to anyone. But who can *I* talk to? What evidence do you have?" She didn't know what bothered her more, that she'd been caught completely off guard, or that her client was silently and without protest allowing the officers to cuff him and lead him out the door.

Detective Cook looked her over and said firmly, "Your client is a murderer, Miz...?"

"Hollis Morgan," she answered quickly. "So you've mistakenly pointed out. How is he linked to this murder?"

"Did he tell you about the Nike bag he *said* he found?" Cook stepped aside for his deputy to pass through with his prisoner. "Fields' murder was reported yesterday. When our officers went through the Nike bag, they found several pieces of Fields' identification. We got a warrant this morning to search his apartment, and we found more IDs that don't belong to Mr. Eastland. Eastland's prints are the only ones on the bag *and* the IDs, and that's why we have your client nailed as the killer."

FOUR

PACING BACK AND forth in the small sitting area in Gordon's office, Hollis waited with ill-concealed impatience for him to finish his call. She halted in front of his desk when she heard him click off.

"Sorry." Gordon pointed toward the chair in front of his desk. "Okay, go through what happened again."

Sitting on the edge of the chair, she described the interview with Justin and his surprise arrest. "I told Eastland we'd be getting back in touch once we talked with the DA's office. I knew...." She stopped speaking and slammed her back into the chair in disgust when Gordon's phone rang, and after glancing at the screen, he picked it up.

"Hey, Steve," Gordon said. "What's going on? Uh-huh, you better believe that's why I called you. Uh-huh, well, I put our best attorney on this, and she was blindsided."

Hollis perked up. If her gut instinct proved correct, Steve was Steve Florin, *the* District Attorney.

"Uh-huh," he continued with his call, but he'd grabbed a pen and was scribbling notes. "Will do. What's the address? I'll meet you there at five o'clock. Don't be late."

She raised her eyebrows. "Gordon, was that Steve Florin? You're going to meet with him later today about the Eastland matter? Can I come with you?"

He frowned. "What? Yeah, that was Florin. Listen, about your client, he's going to be assigned an assistant DA on the case, a Gil Tunney. I met him at a reception once. He's all right. He'll meet with you this afternoon." He handed over the piece of paper with his notes. "Florin and I are going to meet for drinks later on."

"How'd you find out about Eastland's arrest so quickly?" Hollis asked.

"I've got friends in the department," he said. "Don't worry; you'll develop a circle of friends, too."

"I'm not worried."

"Good, then let's meet first thing in the morning, after both of us have gotten more information, and discuss how you're going to proceed." He returned his attention to the message screen on his phone.

HOLLIS HAD BEEN to the DA's office a few times but never on an official visit to represent a client. The offices were located in a cluster of government buildings near the downtown business district. A three-story facility, it had muted brown wall-to-wall carpeting and inexpensive blinds and drapes covering the windows. At the end of a short hallway, a dark oak reception desk from the 1970s guarded two glass doors on either side. A woman, gray-haired and pudgy, peered at her from thick bifocals. Her nameplate identified her as Mavis Thompson.

"Yes, may I help you?" Mavis said in a firm, no-nonsense voice.

Hollis handed her a business card. "I'm here to see Mr. Tunney. He's expecting me."

Mavis gave her a once-over as if running her through

her own visitor detector. "Have a seat. I'll let him know you're waiting."

She pointed to a set of single-cushion foam sofas that lined the walls. Several men wearing business suits sat engrossed, poring over papers or tapping on their cell phones. One middle-aged woman, dressed simply in a running suit, clutched a purse in her lap and looked distressed, as if she was just barely holding herself together.

Hollis took a chair against the far wall.

A young female deputy came through one of the side doors to call the woman forward. The deputy held the door open as the distressed woman hurried across the room on swollen ankles.

"Mrs. Lozano," the deputy said, "we don't have a lot of time this morning. Your son's hearing is tomorrow. I don't know what more we can—"

"Please, please, let me show you new evidence...."

Their voices faded as the door closed.

Hollis vaguely wondered what the woman wanted with the DA. Where was her defense attorney?

"Ms. Morgan?"

A tall, confident-looking man, smiling politely and wearing a Brooks Brothers suit, walked over to her with his arm outstretched. She shook his hand.

"Yes."

"Gil Tunney." He pointed toward the door. "Let's go to my office."

The room was cluttered with stacks of files atop a faux walnut credenza. A four-drawer lateral filing cabinet was centered on one wall with paper-covered two-drawer filing cabinets on either side. A row of three tall, narrow windows covered in aluminum blinds cast light into the room. Still, for all its free-floating clutter, the office had an air of professionalism and there appeared to be a method to the madness.

"Water? Coffee?" Tunney offered, moving to sit behind his desk.

"No, I'd rather get to yesterday and the arrest of my client for murder."

"Good, so would I." He reached for a file from atop one of the stacks. "Your client, Justin Eastland, is a repeat offender—"

"He has one burglary conviction as a juvenile," she interjected. "He took a laptop from a fellow student."

"True," he said, inclining his head in acquiescence. "For burglary, but we have hard evidence that he knew the victim, and," he held out a forensic form, "his fingerprints were on the murder weapon."

He continued, "Our deputies pulled together the circumstances. We think on the night of April twelfth your client was staking out Marguerite Fields' apartment building on Juniper Street, in East Oakland. He spotted her arrival and made his way toward her. It might have been sexual or maybe he was just going to rob her. At any rate, she rebuked him, things got out of hand, and he got angry and killed her. He got rid of most of the evidence in her unit but wasn't able to get rid of it all. He fled. We stopped him for a traffic violation, which led to his arrest for identity theft. It was in the processing of gathering evidence for that felony that we realized we were dealing with murder."

Hollis shook her head. "That is really farfetched. What was the murder weapon?"

"A wrench."

"A wrench. What would he be doing with a wrench? He's an alleged thief, not a plumber."

"We found a wrench at the scene with her blood on it. There were no prints—it had been wiped. But traces of her blood were on the handle of the bag we found on your client."

Hollis was silent for a moment, then nodded for him to go ahead.

"The circumstances surrounding his identity theft charges are equally damning." Tunney took a swallow from a bottle of water next to his phone. "I was going to get in touch with you anyway about his hacking." He slid another sheet of paper over to her. "This is a list of victim IDs we found in his possession: credit cards, socials, and driver's licenses, including Fields'."

"This is a real tale you're trying to weave."

"Oh, it's not hard to bring this together." Tunney clasped his hands on the desk. "Eastland was caught with IDs—*caught*. We have witnesses who will testify he knew the victim, and we have his fingerprints. That's not fabrication, that's prison time."

Hollis shook her head vehemently.

Tunney raised his hand in protest. "Eastland was desperate. He was scared he'd been seen, and rightly so, because he had been spotted."

She gazed out the window and then back at Tunney. "Did you find his DNA on her?"

He sat back in his chair. "All the tests aren't back yet. But like I said, his prints were on the bag with her blood."

Hollis gave him a long look. There was something he wasn't saying. She scribbled his exact wording on her own notepad.

"What's the charge?" she asked.

Tunney peered at her. "Two counts for murder, one count in the commission of another felony." He steeped his fingers. "We're going for the death penalty."

Hollis was silent. She wanted out of there; she was over her head.

"Can I get a copy of his arrest file?"

He handed her the file he'd been reading. "This is for you—all ready to go."

She put the file in her briefcase and stood. "I read the prelim police report. When I learned my client's prints were allegedly in the victim's apartment, I was curious. How could you know they weren't there from a past visit?"

Tunney shrugged. "Is that going to be your defense? I understand this is your first criminal case." He stood and followed her to the door, opening it for her. "We've got your client nailed, Ms. Morgan. Sorry you're going to start your new career with a tick mark in the loss column."

HOLLIS WALKED DOWN the hallway to check with Gordon's paralegal for the third time to find out when he would be returning to the office.

"He knows he has a meeting with you before he goes to lunch." His secretary smiled. "I wouldn't worry. I'll let you know as soon as he gets in. You don't have to keep asking."

Hollis turned to her keyboard and hammered out her notes from her meeting with Tunney. She'd meant it when she told Mark that the Eastland case was not for her. She planned on letting Gordon know, if he already didn't, that he could get her feet wet with one of his more straightforward criminal cases.

She was finishing up her summary when Eleanor came to her doorway.

"He's back, and he wants to see you in ten minutes," she announced. "He's completing a call."

She grinned. "Of course he is. Thanks, Eleanor."

Fifteen minutes later, Hollis sat in the chair in front of Gordon's desk as he continued to "complete" his call. But this time, anticipating a delay, she had brought along a file and used the time to look through work papers Penny had processed on probate cases.

Gordon finally clicked off.

"You do attract lightning, Ms. Morgan," he said, shaking his head. "That was Florin. For now, you're off the murder case. We can't assign you a death penalty matter. So, I'll be representing Eastland on his homicide charge, but...don't look so relieved. I want you as my co-counsel. We work well together. Besides, if I know Florin, he'll hold on to the identity theft charges for insurance."

"Insurance?" Hollis asked.

"Yeah, Tunney can hypothesize the crime scene all he wants, but his evidence against Eastland for killing that woman is probably inconclusive. However, if he can prove that Eastland has a criminal bent and is used to violating the law, then Tunney could manipulate the jury into thinking that Eastland was desperate enough to kill."

Hollis nodded her understanding. "So, you still want me to follow up with the identity theft defense?"

"Yep. You think you can handle it?"

"Yes," she said, surprising herself. "I spoke with

Eastland for some time. He's young, and as you pointed out, a liar. But I don't think he's a killer. One thing might work. I can focus on getting him to tell the truth, because he knows he can't get any lies past me."

Gordon nodded. "Good, then I want you to stick with the identity theft charges. Give me everything you can find out about his background: school, friends, and work. The truth, if you can glean it out of him. From what you told me, he asserted the bag he stole was hidden in nearby bushes?"

"That part I believe." She shrugged. "But the rest, I'm not so sure."

He shook his head. "Talk about bad luck: a computer hacker stealing the bag of a killer who's an identity thief. Well, if this doesn't scare Eastland straight, I don't know what will."

FIVE

In the morning, Hollis and John both dashed for their cars giving each other quick kisses.

"Good luck with your first criminal case," he called out.

Hollis grinned. "I think I'm going to need it."

She drove quickly to the firm and just as quickly made a cup of tea and took the next few minutes to draft a list of questions for her first meeting.

Lindsay Mercer arrived ahead of time. Fortunately, Hollis was ready. She'd gathered her notes and was going through them once more in the firm's conference room when Eleanor announced her client's arrival.

"I hope I'm not playing havoc with your schedule. I have a tendency to be early," Lindsay said as she took a seat across from Hollis. "I was anxious about this meeting and wanted to get started."

"Not a problem." Hollis smiled, pulling out her pad and pen. "Why don't we start with you giving me a little background about yourself and what you hope Dodson, Dodson and Doyle can do?"

Lindsay hesitated, as if she'd rather do anything other than discuss her background, but then she smiled and began to explain. "About twenty years ago, I was hired as an account clerk for a good-sized accounting firm in Chicago. I was twenty-four and fresh out of college, so

I started at the bottom, but by the end I'd worked my way up to Director of Commercial Accounts."

"What brought about 'the end'?"

Lindsay reached into her purse as if to get a cigarette, but then pulled back.

"About four years ago, I noticed this one customer would have extreme peaks of deposits and extreme valleys of withdrawals. It was an investment consulting firm, so at first I didn't think anything of it. Call them Firm A. But one of my managers pointed out that another customer, Firm B, had a similar pattern of deposits. Except their deposits and withdrawals were on parallel dates, and were the exact opposite of Firm A. When Firm B had a large deposit, Firm A had large withdrawal. I did a little checking, and the clearing house for these transactions was an out-of-state catering business."

She paused.

"How long did it take you to discover the catering business was a front?" Hollis asked.

Lindsay moistened her lips. "About six months. They covered their tracks well." She glanced around the table. "Can I have a drink of water?"

"Sure." Hollis retrieved a glass and a bottle from the refrigerator in the room's credenza.

Lindsay skipped the glass and gulped down half the bottle.

She continued, "Anyway, I knew that this was major trouble. For a company to run those kinds of transactions over such a long period—that had to be known by people a lot higher up than me. My direct boss was a vice-president in our branch office, and very little ever escaped his notice, so I took my suspicions to him. He came down on me like a ton of bricks—and that's when I knew he was in on it, too."

Lindsay stood and started pacing. Hollis said nothing.

"It took me another five months to link withdrawals of cash to deposits in my boss's account and…to the CEO of the company. By that time, they were growing suspicious of me, and I could tell it wasn't going to be healthy to stay. So, I went to the district attorney, who was polite and heard me out. I could tell he was interested; he brought in the feds who assigned their racketeering unit and recorded my statement on a video. They said I wouldn't have to face my bosses in court. A month later, they put me up in a hotel and filed charges against the CEO, my manager, and about a half-dozen other employees. Additionally, they rounded up the owners of the so-called catering business, our clients, and a herd of assorted affiliates."

"It sounds like a major bust."

"It was," Lindsay said. She stopped pacing long enough to lift the water bottle to her lips and finish it off. "Then, as the court date drew closer, I could tell I was being followed."

Hollis looked up from her notes. "Is that when they put you in the witness protection program?"

"No," Lindsay snorted. "No, the other side had lawyers by the dozen and they weren't satisfied with a video. They wanted me on the stand to cross-examine. I drew the line there, but it was no good: the judge ruled that I had to appear and the feds gave in. It took no time for the bad guys to find out where I was, and that's when they began threatening me and my family. The threats weren't obvious—my attorney said my fear could be read as my paranoia—but I got the message."

"What about your family?" Hollis asked.

"Fortunately, I don't have many close family members. My mother is alive, but my father died several years ago in a travel bus crash." She paused. "I'm widowed with no children."

"I take it you ended up having to testify in court?"

"Yup." Lindsay took the seat at the head of the table. "The feds figured out they had to do more to protect me. They put me up in a hotel, but they had to keep moving me around because my location was always discovered, eventually. Finally, I'd had enough. I had no life. So, I bargained a nice sum for retirement and a new identity. One hour after I testified on the stand, I was on a private plane to…to here."

"And that was…?"

"Three years ago." Lindsay gripped the water bottle tighter. "The protection program worked, and I was on my way to…to getting my life back. Then, about six months ago, I was diagnosed with cancer, and it caused me to rethink my escape plan—actually, to develop a new one."

Lindsay's eyes began to glisten and there was silence.

Hollis cleared her throat. "Is that when you started thinking about your estate?"

Lindsay looked up from her reverie. "What? Oh, yes. My mother had a sister who passed away several years ago. There was a daughter—my cousin, Nina. She lives near Yosemite, in a little town called Ahwahnee. We're family, but it's been about five years since I've seen her. She's good people. She's single and works for a small dress shop. I want to leave her my estate, and she will act as pass-through to my mother."

"Do you think they are watching her, to see if you get in contact?"

"I don't know. I don't think so." Lindsay wrinkled her brow. "They didn't know about her during the whole trial thing. Besides, by now it wouldn't do any good to out me. Almost everybody went to jail or ended up on parole."

"Still, you're acting out of caution and—"

"The thing is I don't want to take the chance. There are one or two guys I knew back then who had lawyers who tucked them away, and they might not want to risk being prosecuted."

Hollis made a few more notations, and without looking up, said, "So, you didn't give the DA everything you knew, did you?"

"No."

"You were afraid you'd give away your leverage to keep the feds and the state on the hook?"

"Yes. They are notorious for their short-term memories."

Hollis looked up and found Lindsay's eyes boring into her own. She leaned back in her chair.

"In the interest of time," Hollis said, "have you told me the whole story?"

"Hmm, actually almost all of it. I'm sorry, I have learned to trust very few people." Lindsay gave a small laugh. "I must be losing my touch. You were able to see the holes in my tale of woe."

"Do you have a cousin named Nina?"

"Yes."

"Did you have a cancer diagnosis?"

"I did." Lindsay paused and gazed at her hands, and then nodded. "For now, I'm in remission."

Hollis crossed her arms. "You don't have to worry about telling me what's happening. You must know you're covered under attorney-client privilege. Because...."

With a sharp intake of breath, Hollis understood.

"Oh, wait a minute. Does part of the half-story include the fact that you were guilty, too?"

Lindsay winced and nodded again. "I imagined you'd figure it out. I never told Mark. I didn't want to shock him. He wants to see only the good in people, and I needed his help to find an attorney I could trust."

"So that this conversation hasn't been a total ride on a merry-go-round, do you really want to leave your estate to your cousin?"

"Yes, I do. And I'm really in the witness protection program."

Hollis took a sip from her glass of water and reappraised Lindsay Mercer. "Let's start over. First, stop wasting my time. I can spot a half-truth a mile away. Second, if I'm going to represent you, I need to know everything. You have a lot at risk. You can trust me. I can't help you if you don't."

Lindsay raised her hand in protest. "I'm not—"

"And third," Hollis continued, "third, who are you? I researched your antique store's website, and you're not her."

The woman's face lost its color.

"Does Mark know?" she asked, avoiding Hollis's eyes.

"I can't imagine he does," Hollis said. "He usually takes people at face value. Like I said, I wanted to get to know you so I can advise you, get a sense of your business, and obtain some background. I was going to tell him after we talked."

"It's not as bad as it sounds," Mercer sighed. "My new legal name is truly Lindsay Mercer. What I look like is open to conjecture." She played with her drink. "Call it paranoia, but even paranoids have enemies, and I have more than my share. Keeping my real appearance a secret was one of my last protective barriers in case my past caught up with me. The woman who fronts for me on my website is aware of my…circumstances. Think of it like Betty Crocker."

Hollis frowned. "I'm confused, because there are too many loopholes in that logic. But, supposing you've managed to keep your true appearance a secret, what is your plan?"

"That's just it, I have to escalate my plan," Lindsay said. "Sorry about my need to hide the truth, but I've had my cover broken too many times. Call my tales another layer of protection. A habit I will break with you." She reached over and patted Hollis's hand. "Nina really is my cousin. She's honest and loyal. She'll make sure my mother gets the money when I'm gone. My enemies won't be looking at her."

Hollis looked skeptical. "They'll see your mother got an influx of money. They'll try to track it back to you."

"And they'll discover Nina."

Hollis raised her eyebrows and rocked slowly in her chair. "How big is your estate?"

"It's not huge," Lindsay said. "Three million, but it's not just the money they want. They want me."

Her face was grave for a moment; then she pursed her lips and released a deep breath.

"It takes me a while to catch on," Hollis said. "And

you're very slippery, but let me see if I have this right. You say you are still holding information the DA wants. Your enemies want to get their hands on you before you reveal more, and even more than that, they want the money you stole. Am I getting warm?"

Lindsay shrugged again.

"But you've told me that you're in remission," Hollis mused. "Why do you care? If your identity leaks out… as far as anyone knows, it's over for you anyway. Which raises a whole set of other questions."

Lindsay smiled.

Hollis sat across the conference table from Lindsay Mercer, eyes wide in amazement. She was developing a new respect for telling the truth.

"So, if I understand what you're not telling me," Hollis said, not bothering to hide her frustration, "you're not dying. You told Mark that. Actually, you just want to get some money to your family." Hollis folded her hands, thinking. "Because the one truth in this whole tale is that you *are* in the witness protection program. It's also a fact that you are withholding evidence from the authorities in hopes of bargaining for their assistance in allowing you to disappear one more time with the tainted money. And if you're declared dead—and mind you, I don't know how you plan to pull that one off—but if you're dead, you can get out of the program with the money *and* start a new life. Have I got it right?"

"That's a pretty good summary," Lindsay responded, rubbing her brow. "Don't think I'm crazy. The doctors won't, or can't, give me a definitive answer about my prognosis. Yes, my cancer is in remission—for now. But they can't guarantee it won't return. I want to make sure my mother and cousin are taken care of. I don't want them to worry about me, and I don't want to have to worry about them."

Hollis's eyes narrowed. "And my role in this drama is to process your probate in order to release the assets in your estate to your cousin—and then you'll disappear, *again,* with the remainder of the stolen money and no one on your tail."

"You see, it's not difficult to understand."

"Tell me, what do I use for a death certificate?"

"Let me worry about that," Lindsay said, picking up her phone to glance at the time.

Hollis shook her head. "No, I'm not going to lose my license by participating in a fraud. I can't believe Mark knows about any of this."

For the first time in their conversation, Lindsay showed doubt. "No, he knows nothing about this." She moistened her lips. "Look, Hollis, I promise you that I'll produce, if not a legal death certificate, an authorized one that won't compromise your attorney's oath."

"That's a contradiction in itself."

Lindsay Mercer glanced at her phone again. "How long will you need to draw up the papers for a trust? I know that the paperwork for the creation of a trust doesn't require a death certificate."

"That's true. But I'm not sure I want your case, Lindsay. I don't like the smell of it, and it appears dirty from beginning to end."

Lindsay looked away and stood.

"Oh, it's dirty all right, but not the way you're thinking." She crossed her arms over her chest. "Did you notice how Mark scrambled out of our meeting at the restaurant the other day? He felt sorry for me. He didn't want to be present when I told you the 'dirty' side of my story."

Hollis was curious, but said nothing.

Lindsay started to pace again. "You don't have to worry about the death certificate, Hollis. I'll get one from the DA's office. They owe me." She stood, looking out the window. "About four years ago, before I knew Mark, I was approached by a federal agent to assist in this sting operation. They were on to me and they were already on to my bosses, but they needed access to insider information. I was told it was a small role and that I would be compensated."

"How did—"

Lindsay didn't turn from the window but raised her hand. "You said you wanted to know it, so let me tell my story." She continued, "My husband and I discussed it. We needed the money to help with a surgery my seven-year-old daughter needed to straighten a bone in her leg so she could walk normally."

"Lindsay, Mark didn't tell me that—"

"He didn't know me then." Her voice choked. "She was so beautiful, and my husband…he was my soul mate."

She turned to face Hollis.

"It was in the summer… I remember the smell of honeysuckle." Lindsay gave a mirthless chuckle. "Funny, the things you remember. Anyway, they somehow got to Jeff's car. The police never found any evidence, but I had gotten the message. Jeff and Emily had gone out for our Friday night ice cream…and they never…they never came back." Lindsay's voice drifted off into silence as tears streamed down her face.

For Hollis it was like watching a horrific scene and

being unable to look away. She got up to put her arms around the shaking shoulders, but Lindsay stepped out of reach.

She started pacing again, and Hollis returned to her chair.

"They thought they had scared me off, but just the opposite. The only thing that kept me from killing myself was my determination to see them rot in prison. The death penalty would be too good for them." Her eyes flashed in anger. "The FBI traced the leak to a disgruntled police cadet. She gave them my identity information." She slammed her fist on the table. "A cadet, can you imagine? She didn't even know me. She did it for her boyfriend."

Silence fell between them.

Hollis cleared her throat. "Is that why they still owe you?"

"Damn straight," Lindsay said with bitterness. "Now, I can't stand the smell of honeysuckle."

GORDON SAT LISTENING at his desk as Hollis took him through the Lindsay Mercer matter. His phone chimed, but to Hollis's surprise, he ignored it.

"I've done some research on the specifics of the witness protection program and how family members are treated, and in some cases, protected." She looked up from her notes. "I want to take this case, Gordon. Once you get past the background circumstances, it's just an execution of a straightforward trust matter."

"I finished reading your brief." He tossed her memo onto a stack of papers. "The background circumstances are everything."

Hollis shrugged. "It's unusual, that's for sure, but I can handle it."

"You think you can handle the Mercer matter and support me with Eastland's defense?"

She smiled. "I go see Tunney tomorrow, to pressure him to drop all charges. All he has is circumstantial evidence and…and hearsay. Piece of cake."

"Hmm."

SIX

WHEN HOLLIS ARRIVED HOME, she put her briefcase on the hall table and flopped down on the sofa next to John's long, lean frame.

"You're late." He put his arm around her and squeezed her shoulder. "Rough day at the office, dear?"

Hollis chuckled. "You have no idea."

She turned her face toward his for a long kiss.

"How about you?" She leaned back to look into his eyes. "How are things going?"

"Eh, there's always trouble in paradise. But have no fear—there is always the proper form to cover it." He gently reclaimed his arm and stood. "I'm going to get a brew. Want anything from the kitchen?"

Hollis frowned as he moved away.

"No, I'm fine." She joined him and took a seat on one of the kitchen-counter barstools. "You seem...tense. What's the matter? Are you in pain?"

His shoulders stiffened, but he didn't answer. She waited.

He slammed the refrigerator door and sat next to her. "I'm not in pain and I'm not depressed. Nor am I feverish, suicidal, or homicidal."

"John, what's the matter?"

"Nothing."

"Please." She put her hand on his arm and said softly, "Then what?"

Her peered at her then took a swallow from his bottle and stared straight ahead. "Hollis, I'm bored."

They exchanged looks. Hollis was the first to turn away.

"Then let's go out to eat." She slid off the stool. "I can be ready in fifteen minutes," she called out over her shoulder as she made her way to the stairway. "Let's go local. Maud's sound okay to you?" Deliberately ignoring his crestfallen look, she climbed quickly up the stairs. She called down, "Remember, I told you about my client getting arrested, well, you should hear about my meeting with the Deputy DA."

He followed her and took a seat on the edge of the bed. Hollis didn't look his way but rushed into the bathroom. She leaned over the basin and put her forehead against the coolness of the mirror. She blew out a series of short breaths, closing her eyes. When she opened them, she swiped away the tears that had trickled down her cheeks.

Coming back into the room, she sat down next to him. "Please, don't."

He smiled wistfully and held her hand.

"I have to." He squeezed her fingers. "I know you love me and I know you're scared for me," he said quietly. "I know it was hell for you when you thought I was...dead. But I didn't die, and I'm fine now." John paused, tilting her chin up so that her eyes met his.

He continued, "Hollis, I love you, but sweetheart, I can't be the man you love if I can't be me. Life is full of risks, and we both have taken more than our share." He kissed her forehead. "But there are a lot of ways to die, inside and outside."

She searched his eyes and shook her head in an attempt to block out his words.

"So, what now? You're *bored. Bored.*" Her voice climbed. "It's obvious you want to go back out in the field." She shrugged off his arm. "You only care about yourself. You left me…you left me to mourn you."

Tears streamed down her face. She brushed them away.

"Honey, I—"

"Cut the crap, John," she shouted. "Do you have any idea how it felt? How it made me feel? Without you in my life I… I was lost again. I trusted you. I… I trusted you to.…"

He frowned and then his forehead smoothed.

"Ah, you trusted me to…keep my word." John spoke haltingly, "You trusted me with your heart, and when you thought I'd died…then I hadn't kept my word to come back to you. Is that it?"

There was silence.

She reached for a tissue and dabbed at her eyes and sniffed.

"When you say it like that, it sounds crazy."

He pulled her to him, and she let him.

"Well…" he murmured, stretching out the word.

She nudged him.

He cleared his throat. "There are a bunch of platitudes I could dump on you right now, starting with, 'There are no guarantees.'"

He looked into her reddened eyes, holding her at arm's length.

"Let's just stick to the facts. I did come back. So, I did keep my word because that's the kind of guy I am." John stopped and looked past her. "But I'm also the guy you fell in love with, the kind who loves a challenge, loves his country, and who loves a certain lady."

"But...."

He touched a finger to her lips. "But life is too short to only play it safe, and I'm *not* that kind of guy."

There was silence between them.

Hollis looked past him. "So, trust comes with the package," she said, more of a statement than a question.

He shrugged.

She sought his eyes and a sad smile crept across her face. "Let me guess," she said, "they came to you with a field assignment."

John gave her a penitent grin, and reaching under the bed, pulled out a folder labeled with his name in bold letters. He put it on his lap. "It's only for four days. I leave next Monday."

She tipped her head back to look skyward and shook her head. "You are shameless."

SEVEN

Hollis drove on auto-pilot as she made her way to Livermore Valley and the county jail. Despite the distraction of work, she couldn't get the conversation with John out of her head. Years ago, she wouldn't have worried about "what if." She wouldn't have had a John in her life at all. Now she was faced with giving up the virtual "what if" hamster wheel because she loved him and trusted his love for her. It didn't make sense to try to hold him back from returning to work in the field. It was his adventurous spirit that attracted her in the first place. It matched hers. She would chafe if he tried to restrict her. To keep what they had together, she had to let him go.

It was not going to be easy.

This time Hollis was familiar with the procedures for seeing Eastland. When the prison guard led her to an interview room down a long corridor, she knew the holding cells were at the end and the actual incarceration cells one floor down.

She sat at the metal desk bolted to the floor, and minutes later the second door in the room opened and a handcuffed Justin Eastland entered. The deputy sheriff removed the cuffs and the young man took the seat across from her.

Hollis nodded. "All right, Justin, I read your case

file. The DA has a fair amount of damning circumstantial evidence linking you to the murder, but that's a battle Gordon Barrett will fight. He is one of the best criminal attorneys in the Bay Area, and you're lucky he's taking your case. He—"

"Wait." He raised his hand. "You mean *you're* not going to represent me?"

"As I explained at our last meeting, I'm going to represent you on all charges relating to the identity theft," she said. "The DA hasn't dropped those charges. Gordon and I will work together. He'll defend you against the murder charges."

Eastland frowned. "Why do they still want me on identity theft? Isn't facing the electric chair enough?"

"That's why there's hope. Their case against you for the murder isn't as strong as they would like it to be. We're betting proving that you're an identity thief supports their case that you are still a law breaker. They need to show that they can use taxpayers' dollars to charge you with something."

He was silent.

Hollis cleared her throat. "Tell me about your background. How long have you been…computer hacking and taking other people's identities?"

Eastland swallowed hard. "I'm not an identity thief. I just found that bag like I told you. I was—"

"Justin, I thought we had an understanding. We don't have a lot of time."

"Only one other time, I—"

"Justin."

He cut his eyes. "Since I was seventeen."

She nodded and scribbled a note. "Explain."

Eastland leaned back in the chair. "I started with

computers. I'm really good at hacking; it's the only thing I'm really good at." He rubbed his ear, pulling his other hand up. "School was a bust, and by the time I finally got out, I needed money. My parents didn't want me around and—"

"Okay, okay, enough," Hollis said, shaking her head. "You can't stop lying, can you? Your family put up their house to pay your legal fees and bail. Clearly, they are good parents and still think you have a chance. So, just remember, the longer you take to give me the truth, the longer this will take and the more your parents are paying for you to lie." She pulled the pad to her. "How about we start over, using reality this time?"

His face turned red. "Mom and Dad put up the house? I didn't know." Eastland put his hands to his forehead and shook his head. "I don't want to see them until after the arraignment."

"All right." She heard the plaintive note in his voice, but she kept hers firm. "Justin, I need you to tell me the truth, not a cover-up, not a quickly made-up story or some rambling fantasy that pops out of your mind. There is a lot at stake here—starting with your life."

Nodding slowly, he said, "I was seventeen. That's the truth and it did start with computers—that's the truth, too. But I was pretty good in school and I went to San Jose State. It was there I discovered that other students not so smart were willing to pay for grade changes."

She saw him trying to gauge her reaction, but she kept her face expressionless.

Eastland continued, his voice lower and slower, "And then there was one guy who was willing to pay a lot for socials and credit card numbers."

Hollis noticed he was shifting in his seat, but she remained silent.

"Er, that was about…a year ago."

"Who is this *guy*? How does he get in contact with you?"

"Er, I only know him as Sam. He contacts me by text." He straightened in his chair, clanging the cuffs against the table as he folded his hands. "Look, Ms. Morgan, I only worked with him twice, and after the last time, I told him I was done. He wasn't happy, but he knew I meant it."

She stared at him until he looked away.

"When was the last time you heard from Sam?"

He leaned back. "Last week, and that was, er, the second time."

"Let me guess: you were working for him when you snatched the sports bag?"

Eastland's face brightened. "Yeah, I was. Otherwise, I'd never need to. Guys always carry credit cards, cash, and bill payments waiting to be mailed in their sports bags," he said in a rushed voice. "I thought it just had the one dude's IDs. I knew I could get Sam what he wanted and it would be over. But, er—"

"I thought you said you *found* the bag?" Hollis said, noticing his 'ers' signaled a lie was not far behind. "You were actually staking out the area, weren't you?"

He looked contrite. "I know I said that I found the bag the first time you, er, asked me, but I didn't know if I could trust you."

"It's too bad I don't know that I can trust you," she spat back, and glanced at the time. "Okay, let's take it from the beginning. There's no Sam, is there?"

"Yeah, there is, his name just isn't Sam, it's—"

"Try again."

"I'm telling you…" he stopped when he saw her expression. He rubbed his forehead, trailing the other cuffed hand. "All right, there's no Sam."

Hollis rolled her eyes, not trying to hide her annoyance. "Let me tell you what the truth sounds like, since you don't seem to be familiar with it." She looked him in the eyes. "You're twenty-four years old, a high school graduate with good grades, and a college dropout. You have loving parents who you give constant grief. For whatever reason, you connected with a crowd, or gang, or dudes—whoever—and started stealing and selling identity information. I think you use a variety of ways to get that information, be it by computer hacking or theft. I also think you're the low man on the totem pole, and for whatever reason, chose to make your living this way. Am I close?"

Eyes downcast, he shrugged.

"Now, unfortunately for you, this time your luck ran out and you unknowingly stole the identity of a killer." She paused. "And this could be the last time you greet the day as a free man."

Eastland held his head in his hands, and in a muffled voice muttered, "Er, I didn't do it, I swear. I didn't kill Maggie."

"Maggie?" Hollis almost shouted. "You knew the victim?"

He didn't answer, and she could almost hear the gears in his head clicking as he searched for a plausible response that wouldn't be the truth.

He rubbed his mouth with the back of his hand. "I went to high school with her. But she hung out with a different crowd."

Hollis narrowed her eyes. "Justin, did you see Maggie that night?"

Justin raised his hand. "I swear I didn't see her, and I didn't kill her."

"But the rest, the hacking, the identity theft?"

He raised his head and slowly nodded.

Hollis picked up her pen and sighed. "All right, one more time. Let's start from the beginning."

SHE RETURNED TO the office, mentally drained, and immediately began researching the judge's jury instructions for an identity theft conviction. In court proceedings, these would be the elements the prosecution would have to prove in order to obtain a guilty verdict. After another hour of appellate review, she had no doubt her client was guilty. Her only hope was to show mitigating circumstances, or more likely, to cut a deal.

The State of California frowned on defendants who stole identities. There was one case where TSA screening revealed nearly three hundred credit cards inside a foil-lined potato chip bag. Fifty of the cards were in the name of the passenger. That was in addition to the thirty driver's licenses and over one hundred blank cards that had yet to be embossed with a name. The scary part came when the authorities got a warrant for the criminal's email accounts and laptop, and the list of hijacked personal information—including social security numbers, birth dates, and credit information—rolled off. The offender was convicted and sentenced to ten years in prison.

One case down, untold numbers to go.

"Hollis, you have a call on the main line." Eleanor's lilting voice came through the intercom. "And Vince

Colton wants to know if he can meet you in your office before you go home."

"Thank you, and tell Vince I'll come to him."

She clicked off one phone line and clicked on the other.

"Hollis Morgan."

A woman's voice, clear and strong, stated, "Ms. Morgan, I understand you're representing Justin Eastland in the Marguerite Fields murder. I know Justin. He couldn't kill a person."

Hollis took out a pad and pen. "I'm sorry, I didn't get your name. Who am I speaking with?"

"I'm his sister, Daijah Brown. Please call me DJ." She paused. "Justin has his problems, but doing bodily harm isn't one of them and I can prove it."

Hollis noted her use of the term "bodily harm."

"DJ, would it be possible for you to meet with me tomorrow? Your brother's arraignment is at nine o'clock, but I could see you right after lunch…say, one o'clock."

"I'm going to be at the arraignment. Mom and Dad are posting his bail, if…if the judge grants it."

Hollis was glad the woman couldn't see her doubtful look. "Either way, tomorrow is going to be a media circus, and you'll want to meet with your brother," she said. "You said you had proof, right? If it's strong enough, it could help Justin's request for bail."

"Yes, absolutely, because…because I knew Marguerite Fields, too. Everybody called her Maggie, and I know who she was with when she was killed. Justin was nowhere near."

HOLLIS QUICKLY TOOK down DJ's contact information and promised to get back to her within the hour. She all but ran down the hall to Gordon's office, but he wasn't there.

"If you're looking for Gordon, he's gone to see 'a man,'" Eleanor called out, flexing her fingers in air quotes as Hollis crossed the empty lobby. The secretary held up her hand, anticipating Hollis's next question. "Nope, that's all he would tell me."

Hollis walked over to the reception counter. "Did he say when he'd be back?"

"No, but I noticed he signed out until tomorrow after his court appearance."

"I've got to reach him," she muttered to herself.

Eleanor said, "Call him. You know, he's never far from a phone. He won't answer if he can't be interrupted."

Hollis nodded in agreement.

But when she placed the call to Gordon's office cell, he didn't pick up. She texted him with their prearranged 911 code. He called her within seconds.

"What?"

"I may have someone who can alibi Justin Eastland for the murder." She knew to go straight to the point.

Gordon spoke quickly. "I'll come back when I finish here. Meet me in my office at six thirty. Have your alibi person available."

He clicked off.

Hollis's next call was to DJ Brown.

"DJ, can you come to our offices this evening?"

"No," she answered, "I can't get a sitter for the kids in time, and believe me, you wouldn't want me to bring them. Can you and Mr. Barrett come here?"

Hollis didn't know if after-hours home visits were to Gordon's liking, but this was a murder case, and she had to make a decision. "Yes, we'll be there at seven o'clock."

She texted Gordon the meeting arrangements with DJ and the address. She waited for his response and was relieved when minutes later she got his *okay*.

EIGHT

THE BASEMENT OF Triple D's building contained the entrance to the parking lot and the cavernous mailroom. The mailroom was reached through a labyrinth of corridors ending in a large open space with rows of long, narrow tables covered with white plastic cartons holding the mail of the building's occupants. Two full-time staffers handled the distribution of mail for the building, but Triple D paid to have their own employee.

Vince sorted out Triple D's mail before making his messenger and mail pickup rounds. When he heard Hollis enter the room, he looked up, and a wide grin spread across his face.

"Hey, Hollis, how ya doin'?"

She returned the smile. In a few short years Vince had completely turned his life around. It was hard to believe she'd met him in a police station suffering from the last stages of heroin withdrawal. He'd been waiting for his mother to be released from her own drug arrest internment. Thin, scraggly, and homeless, he'd triggered some slim note of compassion, and she found herself reaching out to him. He, in turn, had latched on to her like a life preserver. She helped him get clean and find a job, and then watched him determinedly finish high school and finally community college.

In return, he'd helped her rediscover her humanity.

Now he was healthy, mentally and physically, and the transformation was complete.

"Eleanor said you wanted to see me," she said.

"Ah, you didn't have to come down here. I was coming upstairs. It wasn't that important."

She leaned against one of the tables and gave a little dismissive wave. "I needed to get out of my office. It was making me crazy. What's going on?"

At twenty-three, he could still blush, and a rush of red crept up to his towhead hairline.

"I…ah…wanted to know if you'd come to my graduation," he said, eyes fixed on his shoes. "It's in May, but I know you're super busy, and I…ah, wouldn't be graduating but for you. So, I…ah, didn't have anyone else to ask, and…."

She laughed and held up her hand. "Hey, buddy, you mean I'm your last resort?"

"Oh, no, I didn't mean it that way," he stammered. "It's just that they give us three tickets, and you were the only one who… I mean, there's no one I would want to be there more." He looked into her eyes. "But I know you're busy with this new case and John and everything, so if you can't, it's okay. But I wanted to ask you. You're still my friend."

Hollis turned away from his words.

She spoke softly, "What about your mother?"

"I don't think she's going to be around much longer," he murmured, crossing his arms over his chest and returning his gaze to his shoes. "She's at Highland Hospital in Oakland. She's in and out of consciousness. They said they didn't think she'll pull through from this last binge. It was too hard on her heart and…she doesn't seem to want to live, not even for me."

He choked on these last words, and Hollis knew he was trying to hold himself together.

She resisted the urge to put her arm around his shoulder. He would hate her show of sympathy. She had never met Vince's mother; he'd never wanted her to.

"I'm so sorry to hear about your mom," she said. "I would be honored to attend your graduation ceremony. Leave me a note with the details." She sat on a stool next to one of the sorting tables. "Have you decided what you're going to do after graduation?"

He gave her a shy smile. "I've applied to the Bay Area Investigative School in Burlingame because they have a reputable private detective program."

"A private detective," she said with raised eyebrows. "What put that idea into your head?"

He paced back and forth among the tables holding the white mail crates.

"Ever since I worked with you on solving the Bell case, it's been on my mind. Remember how I staked out that woman's house and…and then I followed that guy to find out where he really lived?"

"What I remember most is you not checking in at the time we agreed on and me becoming a basket case until you did." Hollis frowned, and then smiled. "But yes, I do remember that you seemed to be having a good time."

He stopped pacing and stood in front of her. "I did have a time, and I realized that I was really good at it. So, anyway, I started looking into what it takes to become a private detective." He took a deep swallow. "And I kinda think that this is what I want to do."

She gave a slight shrug. "You know what? I think you'd be a pretty good detective. You certainly have the

creative problem-solving aspect down. Is there anything
I can do to help?"

He nodded. "I'm going to need a recommendation
letter to go with my application. Will you write me one?
You've got to mail it. I don't get to see it. I'm going to
need it by the end of next week. That's the application
deadline."

"Of course, I'll write a letter." Hollis smiled. "I'll
get it done by tomorrow. What—"

Her phone buzzed. She glanced at the reminder.

"Got to go." She slid off the stool. "Gordon and I
have a late meeting this evening, and I need to do a little research." As she walked toward the door, she said
over her shoulder, "Email me the info for the recommendation letter as soon as you can."

"Thanks, Hollis."

Vince walked her to the elevator.

She looked at him. "About your mom—"

"I've got it under control." He stopped her, eyes pool-
ing slightly. "She's gone to me, Hollis. I have to remember that she would be the first to tell me to get on with
my life. She...she made me promise to let her go when
the time came." This time he couldn't stop the little
sob that escaped.

Hollis pretended not to notice. The elevator arrived.
She stepped in, then hit the button to keep the door
from closing.

"Still, if there's anything I can do...." She let the
sentence drift into the unsaid.

With a slight shake of the head, he turned toward the
mailroom. She continued to hold the elevator button.

"Vince, why don't you come with me to the Fallen
Angels meeting tomorrow after work? You said you

wanted to join after you finished school." She smiled. "It would be a good diversion for you."

He blushed. "You guys are too smart for me. Are you sure I wouldn't look foolish? I only read histories, and I'm not sure I'd have anything to talk about." He looked down at his feet. "And…and my background. I'm not as…as sophisticated."

"Are you kidding me?" Hollis chuckled. "We're ex-cons and no better than you."

He grinned. "You know, I keep forgetting about that." He ran his hand through his hair, and then nodded. "Yeah, maybe I will."

HOLLIS WENT BACK to her desk and hastily drafted Vince's recommendation letter. It was better to get it out of the way, so she could concentrate on the Mercer Trust and Eastland's defense. She went through it a couple times and then saved it so she could mail it as soon as she received the instructions from Vince.

She leaned back in her chair and closed her eyes.

"Napping on the job, Hollis?"

Gordon leaned against the door, a smug but understanding smile on his face.

Hollis inclined her head in acknowledgment. "Sometimes I do my best strategizing by *not* thinking." She patted the file in front of her. "I was finalizing my notes on DJ Brown. Other than Justin, the family seems pretty normal."

"Good, then let's go and hear what she has to say."

DAIJAH "DJ" BROWN LIVED in the Bay Area suburb of Brentwood near Livermore. Hollis remembered that years ago, the now refined Livermore had been known for its annual rodeo. Her family never ventured there but a Fallen Angel, Richard Kleh, had grown up in the town, and he would reminisce about the area with its two or three rancher bars and a feed and grain store. It was the expansion of the Lawrence Livermore Laboratory, the national scientific facility nestled in the valley, alongside the best white wine vineyards in the region, that brought jobs and housing. The lab changed the landscape from sleepy town to technical-support powerhouse for its sister laboratory in Berkeley.

Today, Hollis could barely believe her eyes. Coming to the crest of the hills that dropped down into Livermore Valley, she could see in the distance that the laboratory had grown to consume even more acreage. High-end homes dotted the foothills, and row after row of vines carpeted the valley floor. The former rural area had become a metropolis to rival anything in the Bay Area.

Brown resided in Elmwood, a complex of low-rise townhomes along Highway 580, across from the roadway that led to the lab. Gordon, who'd asked Hollis to drive so he could continue to send text messages, pointed to a unit in the center of a circle of identical houses that bordered a moderate-sized manmade pond.

"According to the house numbers, that blue one on the corner is hers." He turned to look around. "Place reminds me of *The Stepford Wives*."

Hollis grinned, noticing the same architectural designs against similarly landscaped front yards. "I agree," she said. "Their homeowners' association must be a force."

DJ Brown answered the door on their first ring.

"Thank you for coming here." After introductions,

she ushered them past a small foyer into a compact living room area.

Hollis sat next to Gordon on the sofa, and across from them, DJ perched on the edge of an early-American rocking chair. With her hands clenched between her knees, she looked like a compressed coil ready to spring.

"Mrs. Brown," Gordon said in his calmest of voices, "you called about providing an alibi for your brother. You said you knew Marguerite Fields. What can you tell us about her?"

"I'm a Miz, and call me DJ. I'm divorced now." DJ went on, "I knew Marguerite, and like I said, we all called her Maggie, from in high school. She wasn't real popular, but she had a few friends. She and I got along okay. When we were in tenth grade together, she was a gawky kid with glasses. By our senior year, the ugly duckling had turned into a swan. She filled out in all the right places, ditched the glasses for contact lenses, and put highlights and extensions in her hair."

"How did she handle her transformation?" Hollis asked.

DJ gave her a knowing smile. "Not well. She turned into a real bitch."

Gordon was shifting in his seat the way he did when his phone was vibrating. She tightened her lips against a slow grin, knowing he was in torment from wanting to look at the screen.

He seemed to read her mind and crossed his arms in front of his chest. "Ms. Brown… DJ, I take it this change in Ms. Fields made her more popular with the boys but less so with the girls."

DJ shook her head. "No, she was pretty ugly to everybody. You see, for her it was payback time."

"How did she pay her classmates back?" Hollis asked, looking up from scribbling notes.

DJ shifted to the edge of the chair. "Well, she started with the guys. She stole other girls' boyfriends. They were so dumb, they didn't catch on until it was too late. 'Cause now she looked like a prize. Then she dumped them after she used them for whatever she wanted— usually money, and she never paid them back. With the girls, she spread gossip, most of it lies. Well, I wasn't surprised when she went after Justin. He had already graduated, but she'd be coming to the house all the time wearing shorter and shorter skirts. He never had a real girlfriend, and I couldn't tell him anything bad about her. He wouldn't listen."

"Did they argue?" Hollis asked, hiding her anger at Justin's lie.

"No, that requires a conversation. It didn't last that long." DJ gave a mirthless laugh. "She used him and then dumped him, just like the rest. I'd say the whole thing lasted less than two months."

"Excuse me, but I'm filling in a witness form. How old are you?" Gordon had the beginnings of a frown on his face.

"Twenty-two," DJ responded. "I know I look older. It's because of the kids."

Hollis asked, "How many do you have?"

"Just the two. Gracie's three and Lola's one."

"Sorry for the interruption, go ahead," Gordon said.

DJ did a one-sided shoulder shrug. "Their father, Lonnie, left right after Lola was born." She straightened her back. "That's how I know Justin didn't kill Marguerite."

Gordon didn't try to hide his frown. "I'm sorry, but

I don't follow you. How does your boyfriend leaving you a year ago exonerate your brother?"

"'Cause Maggie took Lonnie from me," she said. "Justin was here the night Maggie died. He was helping me fill out the paperwork for child support. Month after month, Lonnie said he was going to help me with money. But she never left him with any money. And then she—"

"DJ, how do you know what time Marguerite Fields died?" Hollis interrupted.

The young woman blanched. "What?"

Gordon gave Hollis the nod to proceed.

"I mean, it wasn't in the papers," Hollis said. "The police only released the news that the murder took place last Sunday, and they didn't give the time of day. How do you know it was when Justin was visiting you?"

DJ tilted her head as if listening for a sound.

"Just a minute, I think I hear Lola. I'll be right back."

Gordon and Hollis exchanged glances as the young woman practically ran out of the room.

"Good catch," he said and put his notepad in his briefcase. "However, it doesn't matter if she's lying or not. We can't use her."

"Why not?" Hollis insisted. "Okay, maybe we can't use her to give Eastland an alibi, but she can help with revealing Fields' character and the fact that there are a few people who'd like to see her silenced."

She saw from his expression that he was considering her words.

"Let me think on it."

"Okay. Well, do you see any problem with me approaching the DA with a plea bargain on the identity theft charges? Justin's already admitted guilt to me."

"I doubt if you'll be successful. Tunney thinks he's got a viable suspect on both charges. He's not going to walk away from Eastland without having another plausible suspect." Gordon clasped his hands. "But we may be able to use DJ's tale as our backdoor approach to find out what gives them so much confidence about their case."

"What about putting DJ Brown on the stand at all?"

Gordon thought a moment, and then said, "We'll keep her on the witness list, but not for the arraignment." He picked up his phone and glanced at the time. "I've got to send a couple of texts. I'll wait in the car. You can finish up with her, but make it fast. I need to get back to the office."

The front door had just closed behind him when DJ returned with a wide-eyed Lola in her arms. Briefcase in hand, Hollis stood and made her way to the front door, answering DJ's unasked question.

"He had to take a call. We both need to return to the office to make sure we're ready for tomorrow." Hollis turned to face the young woman. "Do you know any of Justin's friends? Anyone who could talk to us about his character, or his habits…maybe his hangouts?"

Clearly DJ was relieved that she didn't have to defend her well-intentioned lie. Knitting her brow, she said, "Well, there's Phil… Phillip Carson. He went to high school with Justin, and they're pretty good friends. He lives in San Lorenzo, in an apartment down the street from Southland Mall. He can tell you about Justin. Is that what you mean?"

"That's exactly what I mean. Do you have his address or phone number?"

"I know his phone number, 'cause Justin was over

there a lot." DJ shifted Lola. "Do you have a pen and paper?"

Hollis wrote down the information, putting it in her briefcase.

"Thank you for speaking with us," she said over her shoulder. "We'll weigh what you told us with our defense strategy. While we may not be able to use it for the arraignment, we'll likely need it if we go to trial."

DJ juggled the baby, and with her free hand, lightly touched Hollis's arm. "I didn't think Justin would have to go to trial if he had an alibi."

Hollis wrinkled her nose. "The DA won't accept an alibi he hasn't checked out first. Be prepared for your brother to be held over for trial. However, he should be able to get bail. There are no guarantees, but we're building a solid defense plan."

Hollis stepped outside. DJ backed away, looking uncertain, and shut the door.

NINE

THE HEARING WENT QUICKLY. Standing between Gordon and Hollis, Justin faced the bench with his head down.

The judge read the charges aloud and then spoke to the defense. "Justin Eastland, how do you plead?"

Justin, still not raising his head, said, "Not guilty, your honor."

"Your honor, my client requests bail," Gordon interjected. "He's already been incarcerated for several days. He will be living at home. His roots are here, so he's not a flight risk."

Tunney jumped up. "Your honor, the people ask that you deny bail. This could be a death penalty case, and the severity of the crime warrants restraint."

The judge looked from one man to the other, then down at the file. "The court denies bail."

Gordon cleared his throat. "Then, your honor, we would ask for the earliest possible court date, because my client is innocent, and we will not need much time to prove that innocence."

Hollis, sitting on the other side of Justin, could hear a poorly smothered cough from the prosecutor's table.

The judge looked over his glasses at the court clerk, and after some back-and-forth checking, settled on a date. Justin would be held over for trial. Hollis could hear his mother choke back a sob, and a long-ago remembrance of being in a similar situation flashed forward from her memory. Gordon cast a "game on" look at the prosecutor's table.

"I will hear motions in three weeks, on May fifth," the judge said. His gavel came down hard.

A solemn Justin said goodbye to his tearful parents, and a deputy sheriff held him firmly by the upper arm, leading him to a side door and back to his cell. Gathered in a small visitors' room, Hollis and Gordon took turns explaining to his family what would happen next.

Gordon concluded, "But uppermost, Hollis and I will be working hard to get Justin released as soon as possible."

The group left the courthouse in silence. For the first time, Hollis realized what a toll her own imprisonment must have taken on her family. Gordon glanced at his phone and said he was not returning to the firm and would see her Monday.

"Get some rest this weekend," he said. "Have some fun, because starting next week, we'll be doing double-duty to free our client."

Hollis headed back to Triple D. She closed the door to her office, and for the remainder of the afternoon quietly researched cases.

"UH, HOLLIS, YOU'RE SURE it's okay if I come, right?" Vince asked.

"That's the third time you've asked me in the last hour," she responded. "I'm telling you it's all right. Gene knows you're coming, and except for one new member, everybody already knows you."

They got out of her car and walked rapidly to the entrance of San Lucian Library's community room. Hollis paused before opening the door.

The Fallen Angels Book Club had gone through a lot in the few short years since it began with seven members. Membership required a love of books and the successful completion of parole after serving time in prison for a white-collar crime. But the members had barely dealt with facing society again when they became suspects in a murder—with Hollis leading the list. It had been a torturous few months, their pasts exposed to the world, but they'd come through it no worse off. Still, the members were wary, and the gatherings stopped for a bit, until they reunited to find the person who killed their mutual mentor. Once the mystery was solved, they reinstated their monthly meetings of discussing books and sharing views. It was a good group.

Hollis hadn't attended since John's brush with death. Vince nudged her arm. "We goin' in?"

To her surprise, everyone was already there, even Rena, who was habitually late. There was a brief halt to the conversation when she entered the room, and then they all applauded. Gene stood to give her a hug.

"We missed you," he said and turned to Vince. "Hey, man, it's good to see you, too. Welcome to our humble group."

Gene Donovan was one of the founding members of the Fallen Angels Book Club. A columnist for a local paper, he was gay, good looking, and the newly elected president. Hollis gave him a squeeze and motioned for Vince to sit wherever he wanted.

"You know, just because you didn't attend for three months, you still owe dues," Richard Kleh chided, standing to give Hollis a hug as well. "But we'll give you a break for now."

Richard hadn't changed. He was still a money-conscious tease. His prematurely bald crown dipped to let her know he was joking, at least a little.

Rena shook her head at Vince. "We don't collect dues. Richard, who has appointed himself our treasurer, has been trying to convince us to pay upfront for refreshments." She fluttered her fingers. "Needless to say, we ignore him."

Hollis laughed. "Well, I guess I haven't been gone that long."

"I missed you, too," said a voice she knew only too well.

"Hi, Miller," Hollis said. "It's been a little while, but I'm glad to be back."

Miller Thornton was a nebbishy guy—a stereotypical library fact-checker, which he was. His temples seemed slightly grayer and his glasses appeared to perch on his nose for one reason—so he could peer over them. But he had the same youthful face, and judging by the stack of paper cranes already growing in front of him, he was still an origami fanatic.

Hollis took the seat next to him. She glanced around the room until her gaze settled on a young woman seated on the other side of Richard.

"I'm sorry. I heard we had a new member, and that must be you." Hollis reached out her hand. "I'm not the only one who brought a recruit, and I'm glad we're getting new blood."

"Oh, Hollis and Vince, I'm remiss," said Gene. "I need to introduce our newest member—or she was before Vince finally made up his mind to join us. This is Katie Sagar."

Katie was attractive, of medium height and slender build, with dark hair worn in a low ponytail. However, it was her eyes that caught your attention; they were a striking hazel, with a depth of sadness that took your breath away. Hollis knew that look—those eyes reflected betrayal and a wound not yet healed. She saw herself, just out of prison.

"Hello, Katie." She held out her hand. "This is our newest member, Vince Colton." Hollis nodded toward Vince, who sat on the other side of her.

Katie smiled. "Hi, Hollis." She turned to Vince. "Hi."

When Vince didn't respond, Hollis peered at him. He was unabashedly staring.

"Yo, Vince," Richard called out.

It was enough to jar him out of his trance. He blushed as he noticed the faces turned in his direction.

"Uh…uh…hi," he stammered. "I'm Vince Colton."

He blushed at the snickering around the room.

Hollis turned away, not wanting him to see her knowing smile. "Well, now we're back to our original numbers."

Miller picked up a near-transparent piece of tissue and started folding. "We've hung in there. After Jeffrey died, the best tribute we could give him was to keep up his good work."

Richard patted the book in front of him. "So, let's get to it."

The next hour and a half went quickly. Hollis had a bone to pick with Rena, who'd kept Katie's presence a secret. But her friend must have felt the boring eyes in the back of her head and would not turn to face her. Katie was not only articulate, but she argued for her position extremely well. Once he recuperated from his tongue-tied episode, Vince also jumped in. It surprised

Hollis to learn that he'd read tonight's book in one of his classes. Only Hollis was largely silent.

Gene whispered in her ear, "You okay?"

She looked around and nodded. "I was just thinking about how far we've all come." She lowered her voice. "Katie seems to be a good addition. Who brought her in?"

"Miller," Gene whispered. "He didn't tell us her background, and she hasn't volunteered. So we'll wait until she trusts us."

Hollis looked over at the attractive young girl engaged in an explanation of an alternative theme that had them all nodding in agreement. She tried to catch Vince's eye to signal that his earlier fears were unwarranted, but it was clear he only had eyes for Katie.

Gene must have caught her glance. He leaned over and whispered, "Methinks our lad is smitten by the young maiden."

Hollis smiled. "I hope so. He's long overdue."

The meeting ended and the book for the following month was proposed.

"I've got copies of *Hammet*, Malone's latest book, for everyone," Gene said. "Even you, Vince. I just happened to bring a few extras."

Richard sucked on a tooth. "I have to admit, having you work for a paper that gets advance review copies is a real boon and a money saver." Then he wrinkled his brow. "You're not stealing these, are you?"

"First, I don't *work* for the paper," Gene snapped. "I *run* the paper. And second, your question doesn't deserve an answer."

Rena and Hollis exchanged raised eyebrows.

Miller caught their looks and said, "Some things

never change." He shook his head. "Come on, Katie, let's go. I'll take you to the BART station."

Katie picked up her purse and book and slipped her coat on. The rest did the same.

"Wait," Vince called out.

They all turned to him.

Hollis was not surprised to see the flush that crept up his face.

"No, I mean just..." he faltered.

Hollis took pity and broke in, "Katie, I think Vince and I were going to ask the same thing. We'd like to get to know you better. How about we go for a cup of coffee and then drop you off at home?"

"Okay, sure." The girl looked amused. "But you don't know where I live."

The others were eavesdropping, but inconspicuously as possible as they slowly packed up their things. Miller looked on and waited for the outcome.

"You don't drink coffee, Hollis," Richard taunted.

He received a jab in the ribs from Gene.

Aware of the attention she was drawing, Katie blushed. "Look, sure, I'd like to go out for coffee or tea," she said to Hollis. "I've heard a lot about you. It would be nice to talk."

"Okay, no pressure," Hollis said hastily. "Let's go." She turned to Vince, who had already pushed past Miller to open the door.

"Thank you, Vince." She grinned.

OTHER THAN MINIMAL CONVERSATION, they drove the four blocks to Starbucks in silence. Hollis sneaked a peek at Katie, who stared straight ahead. Her glance in the rearview mirror at Vince caught an opposite response.

He was fidgety. Once inside the coffee house, Vince secured a round table in the corner, and they huddled over steaming cups of tea and coffee.

"Katie," Hollis asked, "what types of books do you like to read?"

"Mysteries, mostly," she replied. "But if it's a good book, no matter the genre, I'll read it."

Vince cleared his throat. "Uh, I like to read, too. I like historical. The book club is great for reading all kinds of…of…books. I waited to join until I finished San Francisco State."

Katie looked him in the eyes. "I finished at Laney College. I was supposed to transfer to Mills, but I wasn't able to." She lowered her gaze to take a sip of coffee.

Hollis could only imagine what caused the delayed transfer. However, Vince didn't pick up on the unsaid.

"Uh, what happened to you? All the Fallen Angels have pasts. What did you do?" He slid his chair closer.

Hollis held up her hand before Katie could reply.

"No need to answer, Katie," she said. "This was Vince's first meeting. He isn't aware of the club's first commandment: don't ask—and you don't have to tell. Everyone's past is private."

Vince's face turned red again, and Hollis felt sorry for him. He could never play poker.

"Uh, I'm sorry. I… I didn't mean to get in your business," he stammered. "I already know everybody's past in the group. I… I just thought…that you…never mind."

"That's because our pasts were considered newsworthy years ago. They were revealed to the whole world." Hollis cleared her throat. "I don't know if the club spoke to you about our…our former members."

Katie nodded. "They did. But it didn't matter to me."

She turned to Vince. "Don't think badly of me, but I'd rather not talk about my time in prison. I haven't told the club members, and I would rather only do it once, so I never have to say it again."

"Hey, of course," he said. "It's not important…to me."

They were giving each other looks now, and Hollis allowed herself a knowing smile. "It's getting late. Maybe we should get going." She picked up her things. "Are you sure I can't drop you off at home? What station do you want?"

Vince stood, after giving Hollis an exasperated look. What?

Katie wouldn't be considered tall, but she had at least three inches over Hollis's five feet three. She stood to put on her jacket. "I live near Fremont—a bit of a haul for you. The train is reliable, and my place isn't far from the station."

"Oh, no," Vince said, jumping up to assist her. "There's no way I'm going to… I mean *we're* not going to let you walk home from BART. It's dark and—"

"Katie," Hollis said firmly after silencing Vince with a look. "He's right. We'll respect your privacy, but the Fremont BART Station is not a safe place to be after dark."

After looking from one to the other, Katie nodded. "Okay, then I appreciate it."

Driving back, they chatted about the meeting's discussion. Katie was artful in her descriptions of the members' views, and Hollis admired the way she dodged Vince's queries about her personal life.

Following Katie's directions, they drove about a mile past the BART station into a residential neighborhood.

"Hollis, that's my building," she said. "The green one in the next block, on the right."

It was an older but well-maintained fourplex. Flowering shrubs nestled against the building's front and foot-high lamps lit the walkway and passages. Hollis pulled up to the curb.

"Thank you for taking me home," Katie said, getting out of the car. She leaned in the open door. "You were right. I wouldn't have felt comfortable walking."

"Until next month, then," Hollis said.

Katie waved and turned away.

"Wait," Vince called out, "I'll walk you to your door."

Katie hesitated and looked toward the units. She smiled an okay.

Jumping out, hands in pockets, Vince strode beside her to a side path leading up to the second floor. He nodded and waved as she walked up the steps. Finally he half-skipped back to the car, where Hollis waited, shaking her head. He got in next to her.

"Boy, are you obvious," she teased.

"What do you mean?"

Hollis didn't respond. She made a U-turn to go back the way they came, and in her rearview mirror spotted Katie's shadowy figure making its way across neighboring lawns into the darkness of the next block.

On the drive to his home, Vince was chattier than she had ever seen him. He couldn't stop talking about Katie.

"Hollis, I think I love her."

She gave him a quick glance.

"You don't know anything about her."

"I know it's crazy." He grinned, holding up his hand. "Don't worry, I'll get to know her soon enough."

"Did she give you her phone number?"

He flushed. "Yeah."

Hollis pulled up in front of his apartment building. "Vince, maybe you should take it slow." She frowned. "She has secrets. Or she wants her privacy. She doesn't live where we dropped her off."

"How do you know?"

"When we pulled away, I saw her cross over to some nearby buildings." She shook her head. "And before you ask, I don't know which one."

Vince shrugged. "Doesn't matter. I'll call her and find out."

She started to lay her hand on his arm, but stopped midair when he stiffened. "You may need to give her space. She's only been off parole a little while. I remember from my own time after getting out...opening up to others was the last thing I wanted to do."

"Not everybody is like you."

He got out of the car and gave her a short wave.

"Thank goodness for that," Hollis muttered.

TEN

THE WEEKEND FLEW BY. Mostly, Hollis and John tackled household chores and errands that had been put off for too long. On Sunday night they rewarded themselves with dinner at a new restaurant in San Francisco, then hit Yoshi's in Jack London Square for good jazz.

"So, you're really okay with me going?" John asked, applauding the jazz trio now taking a break.

"Yes, I told you before," she insisted. "You gotta be you. That's the man I fell in love with." She looked him in the eyes. "I'm fine with it."

With unspoken mutual consent, they moved off the subject to talk of other things, and the evening ended in a truce.

WHEN EARLY MONDAY morning arrived, she didn't want John to catch her staring after him. She feigned sleepiness, gave him a kiss and a squeeze hug, and pulled the covers over her head as she'd done so many times in the past. Only this time, when she heard the lock on the front door click, she ran to a window to peek through the drapes as he slid into the car and pulled away from the curb.

Please, don't get hurt.

ED SIMMONS HAD worked quickly. He caught up to her the next morning in the break room, getting tea.

"Just talk to him, Hollis. Get a sense of the man. It's no small coincidence that a good friend contacted me just yesterday and asked if I could use a dynamite general law associate on a temporary basis. He's out here for a year doing some kind of research for an advanced degree. Timing is everything; and I thought of you." He handed her a résumé. "He's waiting in the lobby. Talk to him. If he seems okay, just take him down to Personnel. I told Maria you might need their assistance. Gordon has given his consent, but won't sign off without your go-ahead."

Hollis's first reaction was to resist on general principles, because she felt rushed. But it was true that with the Eastland case, she was already trying to find time to wrap up Lindsay Mercer's trust.

After giving him a brief appraising glance, she invited Leo DiFazio into her office.

She read his résumé and scanned the numerous recommendation letters. According to his law school professors and his law firm managers from Ohio, he was a walking genius. And yet in the first few minutes of their conversation, Hollis sized him up to be quite ordinary. Friendly and earnest, but still ordinary.

Until he began to prove her wrong.

"One of the reasons I wanted to join Dodson, Dodson & Doyle," he announced, "was because of you."

Hollis did a double-take. "Because of me, why?"

Leo DiFazio, in his mid-thirties, was very handsome, with clear blue eyes and dark hair. He was obviously aware of his physical appeal as he leaned forward on his arms across the conference table. What he didn't realize was that the more he leaned, the less Hollis was impressed. His overconfidence turned her off.

"You're becoming quite a celebrity in the legal world, at least locally. No one else would have seen the potential of dull probate law as the fast-track to the top of the law-firm career ladder and a possible partnership."

Hollis held up her hand.

"Whoa, friend, I'm not that ambitious, and I certainly didn't go into probate law because I thought it would get me ahead." She was frustrated with the heat creeping up her neck.

DiFazio chuckled. "No need to get defensive. I'm here to learn from you, not fight with you."

She tried to smile, but spoke through gritted teeth. "Triple D," she paused when she saw his puzzled look, "that's what we call the firm among ourselves." She took a breath. "Triple D is, in the truly corny sense, a family. And while that family culture makes me crazy sometimes, all of us here just want to do the best job we can for our clients. So, if you want to learn from me, lesson one is be a good lawyer, first and last."

He gave her a mock salute. "Point made. Let's start over. My big mouth may have gotten us off on the wrong foot."

"I have a question," she said. "You were hired out of Columbia by a fairly prestigious firm, then you moved to a much lower profile firm in Ohio and now you're here." She looked him in the eyes. "Why the downward trajectory?"

DiFazio didn't blink, but he cleared his throat. "First, I'm as ambitious as the next guy. But I don't like an atmosphere of 'dog eat dog eat cat' in the workplace. Second, I don't consider Triple D as a step down. I did my research. This is a highly respected firm."

Hollis raised her eyebrow and started putting the papers in front of her into a stack.

"Let's try each other out on a temporary basis," she said, making sure her new smile seemed welcoming. "Will a sixty-day contract work for you? If we're a good fit, we can make your benefits retroactive to this date."

"Works for me."

"I'll get Penny to start the paperwork."

"Penny?"

Hollis put the cap back on her pen. "She's my paralegal—yours, too, now. Come on, I'll introduce you."

PENNY STARED AT LEO.

"DiFazio? How do you spell that?" Penny took down his name.

Hollis suppressed a laugh. She would take a bet that Penny was going to run Leo through PeopleSearch, the firm's background-check software.

Hollis gave her a pointed look. "Leo, Penny will be a great help to you. She's one of the firm's best paralegals—because she stays focused."

DiFazio rose to the occasion. He spelled out his name and lowered his voice to a Barry White bass. "I can tell we're going to make a great team." His blue eyes never leaving hers, he flashed a warm smile and held out his hand.

Penny, clearly flustered, stuttered, "I… I…. It's… it's good to meet you." She shook his hand and straightened her shoulders. "If you need assistance, I'm always here to help."

The middle-aged woman could not conceal the blush that appeared on her cheeks.

Hollis couldn't take any more of the awkward scene.

"Penny," she said, "DiFazio's office will be across from mine. Take him to Personnel for processing. Then he'll need you to brief him on local procedures and the court departments that deal with our probate matters. I want him…" Hollis stopped abruptly. Penny wasn't paying attention and had not taken her eyes off Di-Fazio. "Penny?"

He shifted toward the door, breaking the connection. Penny gave a quick shake of her head. "I'm not deaf, Hollis. I heard you." She smiled at DiFazio. "She can be a bit impatient."

Hollis could have sworn Penny batted her eyelids. This was too much.

"She's right, I am impatient, and right now I've got to go visit a client in jail." Hollis stepped into the hallway.

Undaunted, DiFazio followed, after giving Penny a wave. "I'll be right back."

"Ed explained that you're taking on criminal cases." He fell into step beside her as she headed back to her office.

Hollis stopped outside her office door. "Look, I really don't care how you live your life. But this is a serious place of business, not fodder for a daytime soap opera." She leaned against the door jam. "Yes, this is my first criminal case, so I don't have the luxury of time to let you play Casanova. Ed told me you would hit the ground running, and that's just what I expect you to do."

"I—"

"Don't bother," she said. "Excuses don't interest me." Hollis moved to sit behind her desk. "I'll have a number of files on your desk by the time you've finished in Personnel. I expect to have summary briefings with your recommendations for each case by Friday." She looked up at him. "Will that be a problem?"

His lips formed a thin line and he shook his head. "I'll be ready."

"Good." Hollis opened the file in front of her. "We understand each other."

She watched his back as he crossed the hall to his office. She knew she'd overreacted and that he didn't deserve her tone, but he'd given her a smug look that reminded her of her first boss at Triple D—one of the best attorneys she'd ever come across.

She wondered how he was managing in San Quentin Prison.

ELEVEN

THERE WAS A tap on her door. She swirled around.

"Hollis?" said Penny, entering the room. "Can I talk to you for a minute?"

"Of course."

Penny settled in the chair. "I wanted to apologize about this morning. I went back to my desk and realized how silly I must have sounded...and looked."

Hollis waved her hand. "Forget about it. I count on you to do good work, and you haven't let me down yet."

Hollis noticed the woman's hesitation. "What else?"

Penny cleared her throat. "I know you'll need a paralegal who specializes in criminal matters. Geri is the best one in the firm and you should get her. She used to do probate before she got assigned to Gordon. But I hope... I mean, maybe I can still work on any probate cases you take on."

She smiled. "Penny, to tell the truth, I hadn't given a thought to working with a different paralegal." She rested her chin on her hand. "I've always counted on you to back me up. I assure you that I have no intention of having any other paralegal assist me with probate work. In fact, I'm taking on a new matter that could be interesting."

Penny moved to the edge of her seat. "If it's interesting to you, it must be good."

Hollis glanced at the time. "I can't brief you now. I'm

supposed to meet with the deputy DA about Eastland."
She reached for her briefcase. "I'll be back after lunch.
Let's get together this afternoon."

SITTING IN THE lobby of the DA's office, Hollis reviewed
Penny's notes on an appellate case that settled identity
theft treatment in California. According to the state
statute that specified the determination of identity theft,
the severity of the damage or potential damage was key.
Someone convicted of identity theft could face signif-
icant penalties. Typically, identity theft and computer
crimes in general were prosecuted as fraud, and both
offenses were considered "wobblers," meaning the prosecutor had the option of classifying the crime as a misdemeanor or a felony.

Justin said he was guilty, and for once Hollis believed
he was telling the truth. Her job was to convince the
prosecutor that her client had learned his lesson and
would offend no more.

"Ms. Morgan, Mr. Tunney will see you now," the receptionist called out. "If you step over here, we'll give
you a badge so you can enter the office area." She nodded toward a young woman who was already filling
out a "visitor" card and slipping it into a plastic holder.

Hollis pinned the badge to her jacket and was buzzed
through the glass door. Tunney was waiting for her.
They shook hands and headed to his office.

"So, why the call?" Tunney asked. "Is your client
ready to plead guilty?"

He pointed her to a chair at the front of the conference table.

"Mr. Tunney—"

"I'm Mr. Tunney in public, but informally let's move

to a first-name basis. You can call me Gil." He reached toward a tray of bottled water and placed one in front of her. "Now, go ahead."

"Gil, sorry for the late contact," Hollis said as she took out her pen and notepad. "I wanted to catch you before you left for the evening. I know you must hear this a lot, but my client isn't guilty of murder. Every day he stays in jail for a crime he didn't commit is a travesty."

Tunney raised his hand. "Spare me the rhetoric. You lucked out by getting in contact with me today. I'm in court on another case the rest of this week." He took a sip of water. "Now, what do you want?"

She stiffened. "I want the murder charges against my client dropped, and I want his identity-theft charges reduced to misdemeanors. He's a low-level computer hacker, not an identity thief. And as for the murder, why are you so certain he killed that woman?"

Tunney raised his eyebrows as if taken back, but Hollis could sense it was all an act.

"Hollis, the DA isn't going to waste the taxpayer's dollars on pursuing a case we aren't sure we can win. I know you're new at this, but surely you're not naïve enough to think I would show you our hand?"

"I didn't know we were playing a game of 'gotcha,'" she retorted. "There's a man's life at stake. And—"

"Please spare me a sermon," he said. "You really *are* new at this. I—"

"Spare me the insults." She rose. "My client is facing prison, or even the death penalty. I can't be as glib as you. I'm trying to save the taxpayers' dollars, but not at the risk of my client. We'll just see what a jury says."

She grabbed her briefcase and coat.

"Wait." He stood. "Come back. I may have a proposition for you." He pointed her back to her seat.

Hollis frowned, but she returned to her chair. "What kind of proposition?"

He pulled a stack of papers out of a drawer. Hollis tried to read upside down, but the font was too small. However, on the top page, she recognized the federal seal in the heading.

He leaned back in his seat. "An offer that your client should grab and run." Tunney tapped the pile. "For the last two years, we've been trying to nail a burglary ring run by a thug named, Augustus Hammond—Gus, to his buddies. They've been operating on the West Coast. When law enforcement gets too close in one city, they move on. But there must have been some change in policy. We think they are contracting out so they can stay off the radar, and one of their contractors took things a little far and committed murder. We think we can prove your client may be one of their contractors."

"Was Marguerite Fields a victim or a participant?" Hollis asked.

"Not sure yet." He shrugged. "I'm not going to get into speculation with you. But you can see we have a situation that requires special handling. The victim could have been in with the crooks. If so, there's a chance we could bust the ring wide open."

"What kind of special handling?"

"Your client might be able to help us." He locked eyes with hers. "We want Eastland to go public with how he found the Nike bag."

Hollis furrowed her brow. "'Go public.' I don't understand. It was in the press that he was caught with all the fake credit cards."

"But we didn't mention the bag and how it was discovered," Tunney said. "In exchange, he'll be allowed bail, and if he follows our specific directions, we will drop all murder charges against your client."

She was silent for a moment before understanding dawned on her.

"You want to use him as bait."

Tunney ignored her comment and restacked the papers in front of him.

"He will be under our constant protection. We'll be in the wings, ready to make the arrest." Tunney clasped his hands. "Besides, the ring probably already has their eyes on him. They listen to the news, and they know we have evidence that links him to the murder. They know there is a missing, incriminating gym bag."

Hollis did her best to keep her expression blank. She pressed her lips into a thin line. "They can't get to him if he's in custody. Once you set him free, he's a dead man."

Tunney said nothing.

"No, thank you. He'll stay where he is." Hollis gave him a grim smile. "Because I don't think you have enough to convict him, anyway. He didn't do that murder, and you know it." She checked the time on her phone. "Why are you talking to me about this and not Gordon Barrett? I thought he was the DA's chum. I'm just a newbie."

"Good point. Why don't you ask his advice before you turn us down?"

She started to gather her things. "I'm going to do just that."

He said nothing. Rather, he had the amused look of a cat contemplating a canary.

She wanted out of there as quickly as possible. Tunney had just revealed that they didn't really think Justin was a murderer. Or, if he was, they had bigger fish to fry. It was Justin's own admission that had led them to the Fields' killing. The bag was the only thing linking Justin to the murder. So, it would appear that they knew they didn't have a case without it. All they could do was hold Justin for the identity-theft charges, but now they needed his cooperation to trap her killers.

She stopped midway to the door.

"Drop the identity-theft charges, including the computer hacking, and any other felony or misdemeanor charge you've got Eastland on, and I'll talk with Gordon."

Tunney shook his head. "Can't do that. Your client told one of the deputy sheriffs that he'd confess if we give him bail."

"What?" Hollis slammed her briefcase on the table. "Why didn't you tell me that when I came in here? You know better, Tunney. If he did say that, he spoke without benefit of counsel."

"Don't worry, Ms. Morgan." He raised both his hands. "We know you'll be able to pull him back from signing a statement, but it does say a lot."

He was right, it did say a lot.

Hollis didn't need to ask what. She knew that Justin had given a signal to the DA—not only that there was enough evidence to convict him of identity theft, but that he wanted out of jail, badly, and more importantly, she didn't have control of her client.

She retrieved her briefcase and headed to the door.

"I'll expect to hear from you this afternoon," he called out. "Oh, and have a nice day."

HOLLIS HAD CALCULATED correctly that she still might have time to catch Gordon in the office. For once, he was not on the phone but tapping madly on his keyboard.

"Not now, Hollis. I've got a very impatient judge who's willing to entertain my motion to dismiss."

She flopped down in one of his nearby office chairs.

"Gordon, just listen and nod." She leaned forward. "The assistant DA pitched me a deal to free our client on all counts, including the identity theft, in exchange for Justin taking on the role of live decoy."

He stopped typing and turned to peer at her over his bifocals. "I know. Florin gave me a heads-up."

Hollis pushed down her rising irritation and held her tongue. Instead, she picked up her notebook and stood.

"Good thing we're partners on this case."

"Hey, he called after you'd already left the office. Penny couldn't reach you. You can ask her."

"I will." Hollis sat back down. She remembered seeing Penny's call just before she entered Tunney's office. "How do you want me to handle it?"

"How do *you* want to handle it?"

She frowned. "I don't like the idea of our client being used by the DA to do their job."

"But this isn't about you, is it?"

Hollis pressed her lips together. "Okay, I hear you. You think we should recommend the deal."

"Justin Eastland wants out of jail. He's got himself in a corner, and the only way out is through door number one, because there are no doors numbered two or three." Gordon glanced at his laptop screen. "We can't stop him from taking the offer. He'll fire us, or get his family to fire us. All we can do is make sure that he is protected as much as possible, and after this is over, that there's nothing the DA can do to bring him back in."

She nodded slowly. "I get it. We'll put limits on the deal, so the DA's office can't string it out."

Gordon pushed his glasses up onto his nose, turned back to his keyboard, and began typing. Hollis grabbed her purse and briefcase.

"I'll meet with Justin and get him to calm down long enough for me to work out the details with Tunney. I'll run it past you before I get back to him."

"Great. Now go talk to your client. And close the door on your way out, will you? I've got to get this motion written."

HOLLIS STARED OUT the window in the prison interview room, deep in thought. She had no doubt that Justin would jump at the chance to gain freedom, even if it meant having a target painted on his back. She wanted to make sure that, whatever he agreed to, the odds would tilt at least slightly in his favor.

The door opened, and a stern-looking deputy sheriff moved aside for Justin to enter.

She frowned. Justin looked terrible. His hair was oily and his skin was gray. He shuffled even though he wasn't wearing ankle cuffs. However, his wrists were cuffed, and they clanged when he placed them on the metal table top.

The deputy took off the cuffs and Justin rubbed his wrists.

"Just ring the buzzer when you're ready to leave," the deputy said.

Hollis nodded and waited for the door to shut before she spoke.

"Justin, are you okay?" she asked softly. "You don't look well."

He looked at her, his eyes glistening. "I hate it here. Please get me out." He licked his chapped lips. "One of the guys in here told me that if I confessed to a lesser, they'd give me bail. So, I... I told them I did it, that it was an accident. I told them I'd sign a statement if they gave me bail."

"I know. I spoke to the assistant DA handling your case." She leaned forward. "But Justin, why would you ever take legal advice from someone in the same situation as you are? Before we go any further, you've got to promise me that you won't say or do anything that we haven't talked about first."

"Yeah, yeah, okay." He rubbed his arms vigorously. "But this place is making me nuts."

"Like I said, I spoke with the DA's office. They do want to offer you a deal. I told—"

"I'll take it." His head jerked up, and he put both palms on the top of the table. "What is it? When could I get out?"

She held her hand up. "Hold on. It's not a great deal. In fact—"

"Hollis, I don't give a shit. Just get me out of here."

Hollis flashed back to a day when she had been in prison for about a month. A day when she thought she would lose her sanity if she wasn't able to breathe the air of freedom. She had told her attorney to do whatever it took to get her out of there. But there was nothing he could do. She understood Justin's panic. She would have done anything just to get out.

"Listen to me," she said firmly. "The DA wants to use you to flush out the guys who are running a pretty nasty burglary ring. They want you on the streets bragging that you found the gym bag. These bad guys will know that the bag incriminates them, and they will hunt you down and kill you without a thought."

Justin shook his head as if trying not to hear. "I'll take my chances. Ask the DA for protection."

"Oh, they'll *try* to protect you, but know that once you're out, you're fair game."

He gave her a sardonic grin. "Hollis, don't you think they have guys inside? Don't you know that I'm fair game here, too?"

She was silent for a moment. He was right. The criminal world operated just as efficiently inside prison as it did on the streets.

Justin gave a small cough. "Er...there's one thing I haven't told you. I... I've got something to bargain with."

Hollis tilted her head as if to hear better. "What do you mean?"

"I mean, I know that the guys I work with will pay better for some...well, for some IDs over others. So I went through the bag and grabbed the data stick with some files on it before the police caught me."

"What? Why didn't you tell me this the first time?" She frowned. "Wait a minute, how do you know what was on the data stick?" She stared at him. "You took it home and opened it on your computer, didn't you?"

He shrugged. "The police caught me in the car on my way out of my place, not from the murder scene. I didn't have time to check out the files on the stick."

Hollis shook her head in amazement. She hadn't noticed the direction of the address where he'd been apprehended.

Justin leaned over and said in a conspiratorial whisper, "I can tell you think my plan is crazy. But I thought if I stayed here a few days, they would catch the guy who killed Maggie, and then I'd be outta here. But I can't be here any longer, and that stick is my ticket out."

Hollis suspected that her client still wasn't telling her the whole story. But he refused to say more, other than urging her to negotiate an agreement.

His desperation she did believe.

"Okay, I'll work the deal." She stood. "But Justin, you've got to be up front with me and tell me everything, and I mean *everything* you know about this case. No more, 'oh, yeah, one more thing.' Or you can get another lawyer and I mean it."

"You get me out of here, and I swear I'll spill my guts to whomever you tell me to, whenever and wherever. And I'll even tell the truth."

TWELVE

THE PALE-YELLOW LIGHT of the rising sun chased the fading blue glow of night. Hollis stood in front of Triple D's large windows and looked out onto the Bay Bridge toll plaza and the logjam of cars already stacking up like a metal carpet across the lanes of highway.

Turning down the hallway, she saw a light in the office across from hers.

She tapped lightly and walked in.

"DiFazio, what are you doing here so early?"

He looked up from his computer keyboard. "Good morning, Ms. Morgan, you're looking well. Are you asking, why have I been here since five o'clock this morning?" He swiveled his chair to face her. "You gave me an assignment to review our section's open case files, and eight hours a day won't cut it if I'm going to meet your deadline."

"Hmm," she said, looking at the stacks of files on the floor that encircled his desk. "I see you use my filing system."

DiFazio followed her glance "You know, great minds.... Why are *you* here so early?"

"I'm always here early. I like to work when it's quiet and the phones aren't ringing." She looked out his window at the view of downtown office buildings. "And I love watching the light of a new day come up across the skyline."

"Sounds poetic."

Hollis waved his comment aside. "No, not poetic what I am is impatient. Don't let me hold you up." She turned to leave then paused in the doorway. "I look forward to our meeting on Thursday."

In her office, she sat for a moment staring out the window. DiFazio's gesture had indeed impressed her. She was willing to give him a chance to change her opinion of him, but he was still digging himself out of a first-impression hole.

She spent the next couple of hours reading through items in her in-basket and giving instructions to Penny to follow up with pending matters. Hearing the subdued noise of staff arriving, she glanced at the time. She wanted to speak with Justin's friend, Phillip Carson, as soon as possible, even if it was only to leave a message.

He picked up on the first ring with a brusque, "Hello."

"Mr. Carson," she said, "my name is Hollis Morgan. I'm one of the attorneys representing Justin Eastland in a criminal matter. I understand he's a friend of yours."

"Yeah, I know Justin."

"I was hoping to speak with you about his charges, and learn what I can about him. I understand you are his best friend."

There was a pause.

"Yeah, I don't know about all that, but okay, I read the paper and I'll talk to you. When do you want to meet?"

"Would today be an imposition?" She glanced at her calendar. "Say around one or two o'clock."

"Make it one. I got to work tonight."

"Fine, what's your address?"

"No, not here. Meet me at the Golden Dragon Buffet in San Lorenzo. You know it?"

"I'll find it," she said, making a note. "Thank you for seeing me."

He paused again. "Yeah, sure, er...so, Justin's okay?"

"He's as okay as you can be, if you're jailed on multiple felony charges."

THE GOLDEN DRAGON BUFFET was located in a San Lorenzo strip mall off Hesperian Boulevard. Half of the businesses had faded "Space for Lease" signs and the other half were poster children for the perils of deferred municipal maintenance. Surprisingly the Chinese restaurant had a bustling business, and it didn't take Hollis long to realize that its offer of five entrees for five dollars was the reason. The smell of fried food was fragrant but cloying.

Hollis recognized Phillip Carson as soon as he came through the door. He was about six feet tall with a paunchy stomach and pudgy face to match. Even though he couldn't be much older than Justin, his dark spiky hair had already started to gray at the temples. He wore a dark-blue uniform and spotted her as she had him. He walked over to where Hollis was sitting and slid into the booth.

"Hi, I'm Phillip Carson. You're Hollis Morgan, right?" He wiped his hand on his shirt and held it out. "I come here all the time and I knew it must be you."

She shook the hand. "Yes, thank you for meeting with me."

"Well, I don't have a lot of time. I gotta go to work from here." He looked over his shoulder at the steam tables. "We should go get our food. The line is kinda long. Are you going to pay?"

"Sure." She gathered her purse and was ready to follow.

He opened up the paper place napkins to show that the table was taken and led the way.

Hollis loved Chinese food, but after glancing at the various dishes under the glass sneeze protectors, she hesitated. All the offerings looked the same; they all swam in the same thin, pale-brown sauce. She settled on various limp vegetables that weren't smothered with gravy.

Joining her in the line at the cash register, Carson didn't hide the surprise on his face.

"That's all you're going to eat? If you're trying to save money, you have to pay the same for three dishes as you do for five. You should go back and get two others."

She looked at his tray filled with at least six small plates teetering against each other.

"This is enough for me. I'm not that hungry."

"Then I'll go get another dessert." He stepped out of the line. "It won't cost you anymore."

Hollis smiled. "Go for it."

After a few minutes, they were settled back in the booth. A server came up to get their drink orders.

"Just so you know, the drinks are extra."

She nodded. "Mr. Carson, I was hoping you could talk to me about Justin Eastland," she said, chewing on a slightly rubbery broccoli stem. "My firm is representing him. He's charged with murder, and he's also facing several counts of identity theft and computer hacking."

"I know," Carson said through a mouthful of food. "Like I said, I read about him in the paper." He pointed with his fork. "Justin's not that type. I mean he couldn't kill anybody. He's a coward. He can't even stand to argue. That's why he lies so much."

Carson paused then continued, "Ah, you do know he lies a lot, don't you?"

Hollis nodded. "Oh, yes, that I know. How do you know him?"

"Me and Justin met in high school. I transferred to Chabot High in my junior year when my mom moved us here from Truckee. Justin was in my computer science class. He helped me out 'cause I never could understand anything that had science attached to it." He took a swallow of water. "After we graduated, we both got jobs at A-1 Delivery, and then we got an apartment together. That's when I really got to know him. But he only stayed there a short while. He's a neat freak, and I'm…well, I'm not. I like to be human."

"Sounds like you were the odd couple." Hollis chuckled and pointed to his shoes. "I have never seen red soles on running shoes before."

"Yeah, these cost me a lot." Carson leaned back to raise his foot so Hollis could get a closer view. "They're called Louie Buttons; I got 'em at the flea market. They're real comfortable."

"I'm sure." She bit her bottom lip to keep from laughing and pulled out her notepad. "When was the last time you saw Justin?"

"A few weeks ago. We went to see the Oakland As at their opener. He had seats behind first base just above the dugout."

Hollis frowned. "Those are expensive tickets. Did he say how he got them?"

Carson chuckled. "Hey, lady, the guy's a computer

genius. I didn't ask him. I didn't have to. We both knew how he scored them."

"Did you know Marguerite Fields?"

The young man coughed and a spatter of rice fell on his plate. He wiped his lips with his balled-up napkin.

"Hey, how come all the different questions? Don't you want to know about how he uses the computer?"

"I already know."

Carson shrugged. "Yeah, I knew Maggie. She was a bitch...not just to me, to everybody. She started out real nice, then after...well, she turned on you. She got what she wanted from me then she started on Justin." He was tearing his napkin into shreds.

"What did she want from you?"

Carson glared at her. "None of your damn business."

Hollis wasn't intimidated, but she needed information, and antagonizing Carson wouldn't buy her much. She changed her tactic. "What did Justin think of her?"

He seemed to gather himself together.

"He was like a kid. Oh, she went after him all right, then she let him catch her. That's her way." His voice dropped and his face turned grim. "Justin fell hard and right into her hands. It didn't last long, because as soon as he was able to upgrade her credit score so she could lease a car, she dumped him."

She thought a moment before asking her next question. "How did he take it? Did he try to get back at her?"

"Nah, like I said, he hates arguing. He put his tail between his legs and moped for a couple of months."

"Did he do that a lot? I mean use his skills as a hacker to help people?"

"Pretty much," Carson replied. "He wanted to be

liked. He wasn't that into money, not for himself anyway. People used him, and then they cut him loose."

"Justin says he was working for a gang or cartel who
was forcing him to steal IDs. Is that true?"

"Maybe, but probably not."

He looked at his watch.

"I gotta go to work." Carson pointed to the glasses.
"You got this, right?"

"Yes, I'll pay the bill." Hollis smiled. "But just one
more thing. Getting back to why Maggie dumped
you.... Why was that?"

Carson looked away and dabbed his mouth with a
napkin. Leaning back, he turned up his lips in something like a smile. "Look lady, this isn't about me. I'm
only trying to help Justin," he said with more than a
little hostility.

"Yes, but you said she was a bitch to you. So, I just
want to know what Maggie got from you? How did she
make you her victim?"

"Okay." His expression was self-mocking. "Yeah,
yeah, like most women, she had me going in circles
for a while. She wasn't ever interested in me; she just
wanted my free labor and van to deliver stuff for her
and her friends."

Hollis was taking notes, and she didn't look up when
she asked, "Was that after or before Justin got involved
with her?"

"Before."

His one-word answer was delivered cautiously, as
if he were weighing its significance even as it left his
lips. He said nothing more.

She smiled. "Well, I know you have to go. Thank
you for taking the time to speak with me."

He stood and walked toward the door. She noticed him hesitate; he returned to their table.

"Stick with him, okay? He doesn't have anybody on his side."

"Not even you?"

Carson frowned. "Not even me."

HOLLIS STRETCHED AND rubbed her eyes. It was getting late, and most of the firm's employees had gone home. She was tired. Her two big cases were energizing in one aspect—she was mentally challenged trying to stay ahead of her clients. But they were also draining, and she had to stay on top of her current probate caseload as well.

She blinked to clear her head. When her phone buzzed, she glanced at it—a text. She didn't recognize the number.

Would it be possible for us to meet in the Broadway Plaza this evening at 6:00? Katie.

She raised her eyebrows. Miss Mysterious was contacting *her*. Vince hadn't said anything more about her and Hollis hadn't wanted to pry. She wondered briefly how Katie had gotten her phone number, and then realized the book club had probably given her the member contact sheet they used in case of a canceled meeting.

She texted back: Sure, I'll meet you at the fountain.

THE CIVIC CENTER plaza still had a modest number of patrons and tourists taking leisurely strolls and eating in outdoor restaurant seating. A limestone fountain stood at the entrance to a commercial complex and high-end live-work lofts. A three-foot-high sitting wall encircled a public art interpretation of a metal watering can pouring actual water.

A three-piece string band played in front of one of the store fronts, and a small crowd had gathered to listen. Their open violin cases were full of money.

"I used to do that," Katie said, taking a seat next to Hollis, who turned and smiled.

"You were a violinist?"

Hollis looked with interest at the young lady. Katie was dressed in a black turtleneck and jeans, with large gold hoop earrings and a deep-red and turquoise shawl. Her outfit, along with her low ponytail, gave her an exotic, almost foreign air, very eye-catching.

Katie nodded. "I used to play with the California Symphony." She paused and swallowed deeply. "I was in the second violin section."

She stared at the lively band.

Hollis was not an aficionado of classical music, but she did know the distinction given to violin performers.

"That's impressive," she said, subdued. "Thank you for telling me."

Hollis felt a chill. Revelations of one's past were not usually forthcoming from Fallen Angel members. She guessed it must have taken a considerable effort for the young woman to share an aspect of her life that would only beg the question—what happened?

Katie took a breath. "I wanted to meet with you because Miller told me that…that you were a lot like me, and Vince told me that you saved him from a life of drugs."

"Miller is one of the kindest people I know, and

Vince is exaggerating," Hollis said. "His self-discipline and strong character got him through. I'm just a friend."

"Maybe it's somewhere in the middle," Katie said, giving her a sad smile. "At any rate, I'd like you to be his friend and tell him about me."

"I don't understand."

Katie paused, her hands clasping and unclasping in her lap. "I think Vince cares for me. At least, he says he does. I… I'm trying to decide if I can care for him." She let out a long sigh. "We went out on a midnight picnic last night and we talk all the time." She paused and looked down at her hands. "It's moving a little faster than I'm used to, but it feels right. You know what I mean?"

Hollis smiled and nodded.

I'm not that old.

Katie went on, "There's a point in a relationship when you have to tell the person who you are. Who you *really* are, not just what's on the outside but who I *am*."

"You mean the person who was convicted of a felony and sentenced to prison?"

"Yes." She winced. "I want you to be his friend and tell Vince why I went to prison. If I tell him directly, he may try to be a gentleman and dismiss it as nothing, and we'll blindly go ahead with a large crack in our future because of my past, and eventually the crack will swallow us whole. But if you tell him, he'll have time to think about it and decide if he wants me to weigh him down."

Hollis frowned. "Katie, I don't think that's a good idea. I'm not a matchmaker; I'm not even a romantic. Vince needs to hear this from you. He'll have questions, and I'm not the one to answer them."

"Please. I'll talk to him once he knows," she pleaded. "But I don't want to see him when he first hears it. Please, I know I'm right about this."

Hollis had a hard time dealing with emotional people, so stepping in as a relationship go-between would be the furthest thing from her comfort zone. But Katie wasn't being emotional; she was trying to be practical.

Hollis sighed. "All right, I'll tell him."

"Thank you. My story isn't very long," Katie said. "I was convicted of grand larceny and sentenced to two years in CIW. I got out after eighteen months with three years of parole."

The California Institution for Women was located near Chino in Southern California. Hollis had been sentenced to Chowchilla in California's central valley for insurance fraud. A few of her fellow inmates were in for grand larceny, which was a fancy name for common but serious theft. Not including burglaries, the penal code labels it as the permanent taking of someone else's property, the most common example being car thefts.

"What happened?" Hollis asked.

"The professor who I studied under had an original, authentic Amati. It was beautiful and worth over a million dollars, but in reality, it was priceless."

Hollis must have shown puzzlement on her face.

Katie added, "An Amati is a violin. They were first constructed by Andrea Amati in the seventeenth century. He was followed by his sons and more famous grandson, Nicolo. They made the most famous Italian violins in the Renaissance and post-Renaissance era. They are compared to Stradivariuses, and only a few are left in the world." Her voice lowered with her last words. Then she closed her eyes. "One day, I stole the Amati from my professor."

Hollis's eyes widened, but she waited for Katie to continue because clearly her story wasn't over. She didn't have to wait long.

"I was living with a man. No, I was living with a crook," she said ruefully. "I would like to say that he lied to me and tricked me into stealing, but I knew what he was. I didn't care. I did things I'm horribly ashamed of, but I loved him. Or I thought I loved him, and I thought he loved me. He didn't." Katie's eyes glistened, but she swiftly brushed the tears away. "He needed money to pay off a loan shark, and by then we were both being threatened. I stupidly suggested that the value of the Amati would more than cover the loan and the interest. He jumped at the idea."

Hollis couldn't suppress a groan.

Katie glanced at her. "I know, I know, it was terribly wrong," she cried. "I took the Amati when the professor was away visiting relatives. I took it and gave it to my boyfriend. He was skeptical, because it just looked like 'any old violin.' But he was desperate, and we took it to his shark. I tried to explain the value, but they both handled it like it was some kind of…of machine-made toy. Over and over, I kept trying to explain how much it was worth, so he would let my boyfriend and me go, but he didn't appreciate the treasure it represented."

Hollis shook her head. "Let me guess: he said if it was as valuable as you said, the cops would put every fence on alert. It was too hot. He wouldn't get his money."

"Exactly." Katie nodded. "He was a fool. I tried to tell him there was no need to go to a fence, that there were collectors who would gladly pay a lot more than my boyfriend owed. But he said he didn't have that kind of time—that *we* didn't have that kind of time. Then… then he raised it over his head, slammed it against the table, and it shattered into splinters."

Hollis gasped.

Katie put her head in her hands and burst into sobs.

THIRTEEN

"IS MR. TUNNEY EXPECTING YOU?" The receptionist glanced at Hollis's business card.

"I sent him an email this morning." She looked at the clock on the wall behind the desk. It said 8:33. "He agreed to meet with me."

The efficient-looking woman pushed a button. Evidently, Tunney was in his office, and she quickly informed him of her arrival.

"He said to tell you he'll be right out."

Hollis smiled and took a seat. She wasn't the only one who had arrived early to get a jumpstart on the day. Once again, the room was already packed with a mixture of working-class families and suited individuals speaking into phones pressed against their ears.

Tunney emerged with an outstretched hand. "Ms. Morgan, good to see you this morning. We're going to meet in our conference room. One of my team associates will be joining us."

She matched his steps. "Thank you for responding so quickly. I'm surprised you check your email so late at night."

He grinned. "Oh, yeah, you mean your message sent at eleven thirty? You were up pretty late, too." He stood aside for her to pass.

Hollis took the chair closest to the door and facing the wall of glass. "You know why I'm here, Tunney. I don't want my client to spend an hour longer in prison than he needs to."

She paused. The door opened and a tall blonde wearing a severe outfit of gray pantsuit and black blouse entered the room.

"Ah," Tunney said, "this is Barbara Kagan. I'd like to introduce Hollis Morgan, one of the attorneys for Justin Eastland." To Hollis, Tunney said, "Barbara will be assisting on this matter. When she speaks, you'll be talking to me."

Hollis raised her eyebrow in acknowledgment. They shook hands briefly, then she passed a document to Tunney.

"Fortunately, I made an extra copy." She leaned across the table and placed it in Kagan's hand. "This is an outline of the terms that my client will agree to in order to assist the DA's office in apprehending the real killer in the Fields murder. In exchange, he wants complete immunity from any past identity theft charges as well as any future charges that could arise from his past actions."

Kagan tossed the paper onto the table and said in a surprisingly deep voice, "You've got to be kidding. We aren't willing to excuse any future crimes. He's a criminal and a danger to taxpayers."

"Barbara—" Tunney interjected.

"Whoa, what is this, the start of good cop, bad cop?" Hollis shook her head. "You're about to put my client in harm's way, and you want to squabble about maybe someday catching him playing some computer games?"

Kagan's brunette hair was pulled back into a severe bun. She wore black glasses that gave her otherwise unspectacular face an air of distinction and intelligence. She pushed those glasses higher on her nose.

"Who's being dramatic now, Ms. Morgan?" she responded. "Mr. Eastland committed a serious felony and it's likely a jury of his peers will want to see Marguerite Fields' murderer caught and punished. We have more than enough evidence to convince them of his guilt."

"Circumstantial evidence."

"Whatever," the young woman snapped. "The evidence is convincing."

Hollis waved her in hand in dismissal. "Look, I don't want to argue the merits of your case. Can we get back to the points of the deal?"

She turned to Tunney.

"In exchange for being set free today on bail and on his own recognizance, my client is willing to work with the DA's office in apprehending a burglary ring that may or may not be involved in the murder of Marguerite Fields." She peered at Kagan. "Additionally, the DA's office, in recognition of my client's sacrifices, will drop all past, present, and future charges relating to those past acts of computer hacking or identity theft—including any misdemeanor as well as felony offenses."

Tunney and Kagan exchanged looks.

"One other thing," Hollis said. "Justin Eastland is to have twenty-four-hour cover. When the real murderer hears he's out, he'll be a live target." She shut her file. "That's the deal."

Tunney cleared his throat. "Ms. Morgan, do you mind waiting outside for just a few minutes while Barbara and I confer regarding your offer?"

With a nod, Hollis left the conference room. She stopped to drink at a small water fountain in the long hallway. Her throat was parched, and she pushed the lever with a shaking hand, taking large gulps. She headed back to the waiting room, but before she could reach the door, Tunney waved her over.

"Ms. Morgan, we've conferred. Please, return."

"That was fast." She smiled as she took her seat.

Kagan was unsmiling; her lips disappeared into a thin line. Tunney, on the other hand, seemed almost gracious. He spoke first.

"Barbara and I will support your terms and take them to Florin and the presiding judge for concurrence. However, we have some conditions. First, Justin Eastland will be released into the custody of Gordon Barrett. Second, if Mr. Eastland so much as looks at a computer while he's out on bail, he will be locked up for a very long time."

Kagan said in her disconcertingly low voice, "Now, do we still have a deal, Ms. Morgan?"

Hollis's mind raced over possible contingencies or loopholes she may have overlooked. Finally, she inclined her head.

"We have a deal."

"You AGREED TO *WHAT*?" Gordon said in a raised voice.

Hollis refused to back down. Facing him squarely, she said, "First, it's a good deal. You told me it was my case. Justin is ready to climb the walls. He's not the type to adjust to prison, and he might do something stupid. He thinks the deal is great—well, except for the part where he stays away from computers. He's not concerned about the bad guys getting to him, as long as he's out on bail."

"And in my custody," Gordon spat. "Do you realize the ramifications of that obligation?"

"Is that the part that bothers you?"

"Yeah, that bothers me." He tossed his pen on the

desk. "We're not going to be able to control him. He's a kid. He doesn't have a job. The only thing he knows how to do will put him back in jail."

He turned toward his view of San Francisco Bay, shook his head, and lowered his voice.

"They'll use him and either get him killed or catch him breaking bail terms and throw him back in jail." He swiveled back. "It's a lose-lose for him."

"No." Hollis's eyes bored right into him. "I won't let that happen."

"Good, because I'm delegating my custodial responsibilities to you." Gordon's focus shifted to the screen on his vibrating phone. "He's in my custody, but you can be Eastland's babysitter."

WHEN HOLLIS RETURNED to her office, her desk phone message light was blinking. She hurriedly pushed the playback button. Three calls—two from clients and the third from John. She hit "play."

"Hey, don't wait dinner for me. My flight doesn't get in until ten, so don't stay up. Love you. Bye."

Surely, he's kidding.

She used the rest of the time to return client calls. Although she'd moved most of her filings to DiFazio, a few still required her direct attention. She went through them quickly, giving Penny the direction she would need to follow up. Since John was going to be late, she'd be able to spend a couple of extra hours at her desk. Her cellphone buzzed.

Of course.

"Hollis, I got a promotion," Stephanie crowed. "They're making me assistant chief of the crime lab. Let's go out and celebrate."

"Stephanie," Hollis responded, "that's great!" With a sigh of regret, she added, "Can we do it tomorrow night? I just—"

"No, we can't," Stephanie pushed back. "I've got to go to a conference tomorrow. That's why they told me today, so I could show off my new title. Besides, you owe me."

Hollis could imagine her friend's beaming face.

"All right. I'll meet you at Crogan's at six o'clock."

CROGAN'S WAS TUCKED away in the Oakland hills, in the Montclair District. It had been in operation for decades. Good food, light jazz, and a great bartender combined to make it a local favorite.

Stephanie was on her third recital of the day's events when Hollis interrupted her.

"It just occurred to me…what did Dan say? Why are you celebrating with me?"

Detective Daniel Silva of the county sheriff's department was Stephanie's long-term beau—well, long-term for Stephanie. They'd met several months ago, when Hollis had intercepted a text with a death threat. Silva was assigned to the case.

Her friend swirled her glass of Chardonnay. "Detective Silva and I are on the outs right now." Her eyes met Hollis's. "We're taking a break from each other to see if absence not only makes the heart grow fonder but can lead to permanent peace of mind."

"What happened?"

Stephanie took a gulp of wine. "He was using me, or rather, using my skills to get ahead. He started asking me to go into the lab and run results on evidence, so he could bypass his own slow department and get a jump on a case." She sighed. "At first, I didn't mind. But then he wanted me to drop everything and do his analysis—on my free time, I might add. I had to draw the line."

Hollis reached over and patted her hand. "Stephanie, I am so sorry."

"Me, too."

They both sipped from their drinks. Hollis saw the glisten of impending tears.

"So, tell me about the promotion again," she urged.

Stephanie's smile haltingly reappeared. "Well, at least something is working in my life." She played with her cocktail napkin. "My manager called me in and said that they'd been observing me for a while. It was agreed that I was a leader and a great analyst. He handed me a letter from Personnel with my new title and increased pay."

Hollis grinned. "Pay and title, two magic words—congratulations."

A tear slid down Stephanie's cheek. "Yeah, thank you, but the three words I really wanted to hear needed to come from Dan."

"Steph—"

"He said he couldn't believe I didn't like helping him out. He thought I'd want to be a partner. That he didn't think I'd be so self-centered."

"Wait a minute, that's totally untrue. You're a little grumpy sometimes, but far from self-centered. Don't buy what he's selling." Hollis raised her voice. "He's guilt-tripping you and trying to manipulate your feelings."

"But—"

"Walk away, Stephanie. No, *run* away. He's not the one for you."

"Funny thing is, I'm always the one who wants to leave. Now…now I know how it feels when you don't want it to end."

Hollis gazed at her friend. She was the last person to provide relationship counseling. It wasn't in her DNA. Stephanie was right: in the past she was the one who had maintained the upper hand in her relationships, ending them deliberately even before they took hold. It must be a cold bucket of water in the face to be on the other side.

"You know, a break might not be a bad thing for the two of you," Hollis said. "It doesn't have to mean the end. Besides, it frees up time for some forensic lab work I need you to do for me." She struggled to keep a straight face.

Stephanie jerked up her head. Eyes full of tears, she smiled then started to laugh.

"Thanks, Hollis."

HOLLIS HEARD THE key in the lock and jumped to attention on the sofa. She had dozed off.

"Honey, I'm home," John said in a loud whisper.

With a grin, she raised her arms, wrapped them around his neck, and welcomed his lingering kiss.

"I missed you," she murmured into his chest. "I love you."

"I love you, too." He pushed her back to look into her eyes. "You okay?"

She nodded. "I heard a story today that had a very sad ending. And I realized that love—*our* love—should never be taken for granted."

John cupped her chin. "I have no intention of letting that happen."

FOURTEEN

FOR THE SECOND time that week, Hollis sat in the busy waiting room at the county jail. This time her thoughts were on the long checklist of items on her notepad. Finding a place for Justin to live had been tricky, but she was satisfied that staying at home with his parents was the safest thing for him. She'd placed a call and spoken with his father.

"We'll keep a close eye on him, Hollis," Henry Eastland promised. "Justin is basically a good boy who fell into bad company. He and his sister were raised to know right from wrong."

Evidently knowing was not the same as practicing.

She looked at her watch. Tunney was running late. She'd just finished the thought when Barbara Kagan came through the door and nodded for her to enter. She looked flustered.

She spoke in a hushed tone as soon as Hollis cleared the doorway.

"We obtained the court order for release on bail, and they'll be bringing your client out in about thirty minutes. But, ah, there was an incident."

Hollis halted her steps. "An incident? What's wrong? Is Justin okay?"

"He's fine." She pointed to an empty interview room. "Let's sit and talk in here."

Hollis didn't sit but stood just inside the doorway.

"What's going on, Kagan?" she asked.

"He was involved in a fight."

"A fight? He was alone in a locked cell." Hollis's voice rose in pitch. "What are you talking about? And could you tell it to me all at once, so I don't have to drag it out of you?"

Kagan took a seat and pointed for Hollis to do the same. "It's going to take a few minutes before they bring him up, so you might as well sit." She avoided Hollis's eyes. "Evidently, the guard told him to get ready because he was getting out today. They were going to move him into a holding cell, which has less security and saves time when a prisoner is about to be released." She stopped then rushed on when she saw the look of concern on Hollis's face, "Anyway, there was a fight in a transition area—two other prisoners were having at it, and maybe Justin joined in or was dragged into it. We don't know. Fortunately, the guard heard the ruckus and returned before Eastland was seriously hurt."

"Are you kidding me? You know Justin didn't join in. They were trying to silence him before he could get out of their reach. Were they arrested?"

Kagan coughed. "By the time the guard got back, the other two men had disappeared and—"

"Disappeared? What is this place, a circus?" Hollis put her hand to her forehead. "But Justin can identify them."

"He can, but he won't."

Hollis just stared at her.

"That's right. He won't ID them. Despite the punches to his face, he says he didn't see them clearly."

Hollis leaned back in her chair. "He's afraid of the guys he used to work for. They know he's cut a deal."

Kagan nodded.

There was a knock on the door. Kagan faced a grim-looking guard. "Eastland's at prisoner reception. We've got a guard with him."

"We'll be right there," Kagan said, stepping aside to allow Hollis to join her in the hallway.

Justin was dressed in his street clothes and carried a small plastic bag of items. Despite a soon-to-be-glaring black-eye, he wore a grin as wide as a little boy's with his first homerun.

"Hey, Ms. Morgan, let's go." He walked up to her and gave her an awkward hug. "Bye, guys." He gave a tap wave to the guards.

Hollis, caught off-balance by the hug, stumbled backwards a step. She recovered quickly. "Come on, Justin," she said. "For once I wholeheartedly agree with you. Let's go home."

Like a large puppy taken for a walk, he half-ran to her car. In a few minutes they were on the MacArthur Freeway, headed toward his parents' home in Castro Valley. Also like a puppy, he gazed out the window as if seeing the streets for the first time.

"You want to tell me what happened?" Hollis asked. She couldn't see his expression.

He shrugged and turned to look out the windshield. "Nothing to tell. I ran into a pair of fists with a message."

"You know who did this."

Justin looked at her. "If I did, I wouldn't tell you."

She waited a few minutes before she spoke again. "Until you put them away, you'll never be free, jail or no jail."

He gave a small laugh. "I've got protection—something the good guys and the bad guys want. As long as I have it, I'll be kept alive."

"Alive, Justin, just alive, but you won't have a life."

For the next few minutes, she tried to get him to reveal what the "something" was, but he was an expert at dodging her questions, and she knew that if she pressed, he would only lie to her. They drove the rest of the way in silence. Exiting the freeway, Hollis pulled into a gas station lot near the air pumps and turned off the ignition.

"Before I take you to your mom and dad, I want to be perfectly clear." She waited for him to face her. "You're out here on a pass because the DA is using you to get the goods on guys they can't get without you. But don't be under the impression they like working with you. They don't. When I went over the terms of the agreement with you, you said you understood. But it's only as good as your adherence to your side of the deal. You violate any deal point and you're back behind bars with your new, unnamed friends."

He winced. "I said I understood."

She continued, "The cops are going to be close by. I'll be checking with you every day or so, but you call me if you spot anyone or anything who makes you uncomfortable."

He nodded, but this time Hollis noticed he was looking a little unsure.

AMELIA AND HENRY EASTLAND were waiting on the porch, and they rushed to the car to greet their son as Hollis pulled into the driveway. Amelia, with tears in her eyes, grabbed Justin and gave him a firm hug. Looking anxiously on, Henry urged them all to go into the house. Hollis glanced along the street and spotted an inconspicuous late-model white Honda parked a few houses down, near the corner. The man inside gave her a small nod.

They all got settled in the living room, and Hollis explained what their lives would now entail.

Henry cleared his throat. "We'll keep him clean, Ms. Morgan. Do…do you think the police will catch the men who committed the murder? Are they close to finding out who really killed that girl?"

"No, I don't think so." Hollis knew what they wanted to hear, but because she liked them, she decided to tell the truth. "Mr. and Mrs. Eastland, I truly think the DA knows Justin did not kill Marguerite Fields. All they have is circumstantial evidence, but it's strong circumstantial evidence, so they can't let him off the hook, either."

His mother choked back a sob.

"But…" Hollis paused. "But if Justin helps them by…by—"

"Doing their job," Henry broke in.

Hollis glanced down at her hands and then looked Henry in the eyes. "If he keeps clean and stays out of trouble, then he has a chance at a clean slate. And that's worth a lot."

Justin gave a slight laugh. "Hey, Mom, Dad, don't worry. I'm not crazy. I've learned my lesson. I'm not going back there. I'm going to get a job, maybe even go back to school."

Justin squeezed his mother's shoulders. Henry and Hollis exchanged doubtful looks.

"There will be someone watching Justin twenty-four/ seven," Hollis said. "He's parked outside now. And I just thought of another bit of insurance that might give you some peace of mind."

They all turned to her.

"What?" Justin asked.

"Not what, who." Hollis smiled. "I'm thinking you should have a new best friend."

FIFTEEN

"THESE ARE THE folders for the Mercer files." Penny handed them over. "And this is the information I located on her niece, Nina Shaw."

Hollis took the file.

"Any surprises?"

Penny sat stiffly in her chair. "She's forty-six, divorced, lives in Ahwahnee by herself, and works at a dress shop in town. There's nothing in public records that raises a red flag, and she seems to have lived an unremarkable life. How does this stack up with what Lindsay Mercer told you?"

"No immediate contradictions. Make a contact sheet on her." Hollis tapped a few keys on her keyboard. "I've finished the Mercer trust papers. I just put the final draft in your box. My calendar is open for tomorrow afternoon. Contact Lindsay and see if she's available. I'm taking Vince out to meet Justin Eastland this afternoon, so it looks like I'll be gone most of the day."

Penny nodded and stood. "By the way, you wanted time with Vince. He'll be up in a few minutes."

"Good."

Hollis hardly recognized Vince when he tapped on her office door to enter. He was wearing a slate-gray sports jacket, pale-blue button-down shirt, and dark blue jeans. He looked quite the professional.

She smiled. "You clean up good, kid."

He blushed. "You think so? I'm not going to wear this tomorrow. 'Cause no one has friends who wear this stuff all the time." He sat down, brushing at a nonexistent wrinkle. "But I wanted to get a new look. You know what I mean?"

"Yeah." Hollis thought back to an earlier Vince. "Yeah, I think so."

She came around from her desk chair to sit next to him.

"Vince, you know you don't have to do this. Gordon and I both won't think any less of you."

"From what you told me, I would be keeping this guy under close surveillance. Maybe even trying to get him to trust me, so he'll talk to me. He lives at home, and the cops are on him twenty-four/seven. It's not like he can live life in the fast lane."

"There's one other thing," Hollis said. "Justin told me that he's got 'protection.' He didn't give up all the contents of that Nike bag. He's holding on to a data disk. He wants to either blackmail the gang's leader or to use it as leverage with the prosecutor." She took a deep breath. "At any rate, he's playing with fire. If he tells you anything or—"

"Got it."

His light tone worried her. "People have been killed, Vince. This situation could be dangerous, *very* dangerous and…."

He shook his head. "Come on, Hollis. I'm not a kid, and you're not my mother."

She could tell from the flush climbing up his neck that his words had come out harsher than he meant them to.

He gave her a softened look. "Sorry, what I meant to say is that I don't need protecting." He raked his fingers through his hair. "This is my chance to do what I want to do in life, and I'll take that chance."

"Just as long as you realize it's not just you you're chancing," Hollis pushed back, reaching for a folder on her desk. "Here's Justin Eastland's file. Read it and ask me any questions you might have. I'll be checking in with the both of you every couple of days. Don't forget: Justin is a habitual liar." She paused. "But Vince, if anything comes up—and I mean anything that your gut tells you doesn't feel right, anyone you spot too many times—I want you to call me, no matter the time and—"

"And if you can't get her, call me," Gordon said, walking in and taking the seat by the door. "She's right. This is not a game."

Vince sat up straighter in his chair. "Good morning, Mr. Barrett." He rushed on, "Hollis explained my duties, and I understand the seriousness."

Gordon nodded. "All right, then. Let's go through your assignment one more time."

HOLLIS AND VINCE pulled up in front of the Eastland home in separate cars. After Vince had changed into his jeans and polo shirt, they'd eaten lunch at California Pizza Kitchen, where he had surprised her by revealing it was one of his favorite places.

"I'm not a hermit," he grinned. "I do go out."

"I would hope so," she said, smiling to herself. It was another indication that her protégé was ready to move on.

JUSTIN OPENED THE door as they came down the path. He gazed at Vince with more than a little curiosity, matching the assessment Vince gave him.

"Hey, come on in." He reached out to Vince. "I guess you've figured that I'm Justin."

Vince shook his hand and grinned. "Vince Colton."

Hollis turned around and spotted the surveillance car parked across the street. Justin moved aside as they entered the house.

"Are your parents home?" she asked.

"Yeah, in the living room, waiting for you guys."

The living room wasn't large, and with an oversized sofa and loveseat so close together, the five of them appeared to be sitting in a huddle. Hollis introduced Vince and briefly described his role for the short term. Henry and Amelia looked relieved.

"He's been good about not going out until you said he could," Henry responded.

"That's good," Hollis said to Justin. "I figured you might be getting a little punchy. That's why I thought Vince might assist. But I'll need to speak with you tomorrow." She turned back to his parents. "There are some things I have to know about his case. He's still on the hook to the DA's office."

Justin swerved away from her scrutiny. It was clear he knew what she wasn't saying.

"But he's safe now." Amelia nodded to her husband.

She sighed. "Mrs. Eastland, I can't guarantee Justin's safety. Vince is here to better your son's odds when he ventures out that door." She saw the worry lines reappear on his mother's forehead, and she felt the need to give her some hope. "However, the police seem to think that they're close to nailing these guys."

Amelia Eastland gave her husband's arm a squeeze, and Hollis wanted to clobber Justin for putting his family through this much worry and grief. Then, in a moment's flash, she remembered the look her father had given her as she walked out of the courtroom in police custody, headed for prison.

Glass houses.

"Tell you what," Vince said to Justin. "Are you hungry? Why don't you grab your jacket, and let's go get something to eat."

Justin jumped up. "I already ate."

"So have I," Vince responded. "So, let's go get a beer."

He gave Hollis a look, daring her to say a word.

"HEY, I WAS HOPING you'd come back to the office," DiFazio said from the doorway. "I've been waiting for you. I was told you always put in the extra hours. Maybe we could go over those cases you assigned me."

Hollis bit her bottom lip to suppress her vague irritation and an accompanying retort. "DiFazio, I didn't think we'd set a time for today to have our meeting."

"We didn't, but I'm ready anytime you are."

"Well, why don't you give me a half hour to settle in, and we'll meet in the law library. You can spread the files out on the large table."

He gave her a mock two-finger salute. "Works for me."

It didn't take her long to return phone calls and grab a cup of tea. She sipped as she played back Vince's second thank you. Later, she would tackle the inquiries from a couple of new clients and send an acceptance to John for an invitation to dinner at home and a DVR movie.

She smiled. She'd be glad when he got home.

TRIPLE D'S LIBRARY was well stocked. Floor-to-ceiling shelves filled with books lined the walls surrounding a half-dozen rows of tall, freestanding shelves holding legal research volumes and appellate court decisions. It smelled of tradition, knowledge, and just a hint of lemon polish.

Leo DiFazio sat comfortably, reading the *Wall Street Journal*. It irked Hollis.

She slammed her legal notepad on the table. "Let's get started. I've got to prep for an important meeting tomorrow." She leaned back in her chair. "Take me through the Wilson Trust."

Hollis took a little pleasure in seeing him reshuffle the files with some irritation—he had clearly expected to brief her in alphabetical order. To her surprise, he rapidly recovered. Ready and competent, he briefed each of the half-dozen cases with a summary background and then methodically took her through his recommended approach. After two hours, she gave him a grudging nod.

"Mrs. Woods will take up your time with small talk, but she's harmless. Her estate is quite large, and this revision to her trust needs to be made clear to her executor. He's almost as elderly as she is, but I couldn't get her to select someone younger. So, rather than just mailing the document, I was planning to meet with him. Now you can."

Hollis paused. DiFazio had been scribbling notes. He looked up.

"Any more questions?" she asked.

"No, no, I got it," he replied. "When do you want to set up a regular time to go over my updates?"

She looked at her calendar. "Let's make it the end of the week—on Friday. I'll tell Penny to get back to you with a specific time."

Hollis handed him the stack of folders at her side and began to take Leo through the probate clients who she had processed but still had pending actions. He fell easily into step with her, and to her surprise, was quite perceptive and asked good questions.

She handed him the last file.

"I won't insult you by saying I'm surprised by your work," she said. "But you did a very good job and I really don't think there is anything I would add." She ran her eyes down a single-page listing of case summaries. "Speaking from experience, I can say that you may want to give yourself a little more time to secure a court date. Judge Morris's probate court is notoriously behind schedule."

DiFazio was beaming from her compliment and nodded vigorously as he made a notation. "Thanks, Hollis. It means a lot, coming from you. I've got this under control."

"Whoa, not so fast. In addition to our weekly meeting, in the future, I want to see a day's case activity summary every evening before you go home." She stood. "Once we learn how to work together, you can drop it, but for now I need to know what you're doing."

He raised an eyebrow and said, "Understood."

She smiled. "Well, then, welcome aboard."

SIXTEEN

Usually Hollis didn't relish eating unaccompanied in restaurants. She wasn't concerned about being lonely, but she disliked the amount of attention someone dining alone attracted. People seemed to think you wanted to talk or have company. They were usually wrong in her case. But today was different; the presence of a companion would be welcome. She glanced at her phone for the time.

Vince was late.

She rehearsed in her head how to deliver Katie's story. Katie, she knew, was waiting anxiously to hear about how things went. Then she spotted a lean figure weaving around the tables, heading for hers.

"Hey, Hollis, this is a nice place. I've never eaten here before." He sank into the booth's leather seat and picked up the menu. "I was surprised when you wanted to meet for lunch. Twice in one week. This must be a special occasion. What's up?"

"Order whatever you want. I need to talk to you."

At that, he tossed his menu onto the table. "Wait a minute, what's the matter?"

She took a calming breath, her planned speech suddenly a blank. "Katie asked to see me. I… I told her I would help her."

"Help her what?"

"Let's order first. Don't you want to eat? I can talk while you eat." She was hoping his usual ravenous appetite would give her time to pause while he chewed. She waved the server over.

But judging by the way Vince was looking at her, it was not to be. The server left after taking their drink orders.

"What did Katie want?" Vince said, unsmiling.

"For you to hear about her history."

He broke out a wide smile. "Oh, that's it. I thought she wanted to call us off." He picked up the menu again.

"No." Hollis couldn't help returning his exuberant smile. "But she feels it's important for you to know what…what happened to her and have a chance to decide for yourself if she's the right one for you."

"Ah, nothing she could say would change my mind."

She shrugged. "The thing is, it's important to her."

Hollis pushed her shoulders back and recounted Katie's story. Vince listened without speaking and when the server came, they both ordered. After she finished talking, Vince sat frowning.

"What happened to the dude?"

"Ironically, the police saved him. The loan shark beat him up so bad they put him in the hospital. Katie hid out at a friend's house, eventually turned herself in, and got a lighter sentence by pleading no contest. They were both convicted. He's still inside. He committed another felony during his incarceration, so he'll be there awhile."

She was careful not to refer to the "dude" as Katie's boyfriend or even ex-boyfriend. Stone-faced, Vince took a sip of iced tea. They had a few bites of salad in silence.

He ran his hand over his head. "What do you think of her?"

Hollis shrugged. "She seems nice. I think she's telling the truth, and she obviously cares about what you think."

"And I think I love her. I know it sounds crazy, but there it is," he said. "It doesn't matter what she did with him. I want to be with her for the rest of my life."

Hollis shifted in her seat and cleared her throat. "Vince, relationships take time, let alone life-long relationships. I agree with you—her past is past. But before you commit all the way, don't you think you should wait and see if you two are really compatible?"

"Wait for what? Wait for something to be wrong, so I know that I didn't make a mistake?" he said through gritted teeth. "How long should I wait for something to go wrong, Hollis? How long?"

"I just meant—"

"What you don't understand about me is that I would rather have this be the biggest mistake of my life, I mean the *biggest*—and I've made big ones. If it means I'd have a chance to experience love with her for an extra day. I know who she is; she doesn't have to tell me. I'm not going to wait for something to go wrong." His hand clenched into a fist on the table top. "I'm not like you and John. Is that why you don't marry him, because you're waiting for something to go wrong?"

"Back off, that isn't fair," Hollis choked on her anger.

"No, you're right, life isn't fair," Vince retorted. "Life isn't fair and it's too short."

HOLLIS RETURNED TO the firm agitated and dejected. She had tried to tell Vince that she actually liked Katie, but she could tell that he'd been disappointed at her initial response. While they'd both reined in their emotions, apologized, and turned to lighter topics, their parting was strained.

She finished drafting Justin's conditional release agreement, and after a swift triage through her emails, packed the Mercer file in her briefcase as well. She planned to double-check the terms of the trust during her down time over the weekend.

She wanted to make John a special dinner. It would push the day away for a while.

"Hollis, wait," Penny called out as she hurried down the hallway to meet Hollis in the lobby. "I need to talk you for a second."

She stopped and paused for the paralegal to reach her.

"What is it?"

The woman gasped dramatically, "I caught Leo going through your desk."

"What!"

Penny raised her hand. "At lunchtime, after you left to meet Vince, I went to your office to drop off several client letters for your signature. I had signed out for lunch, but I changed my mind and decided to work through the hour. Your door was closed, but not locked, and I went in like I always do." Her voice dropped. "There was Leo, sitting in your chair, looking through a file."

Hollis frowned. "What did DiFazio say when you caught him?"

"Oh, he was cool. He said he was working on an assignment and he needed some information so he could meet some deadline you set for him." She leaned toward Hollis. "But his face was beet-red. I knew he wasn't counting on me being around."

"Then what happened? Could you see which file?"

"Not at first," she whispered. "He scrambled out of

there. But I went back later and figured out it was Lindsay Mercer's file."

Hollis tightened her lips. So much for the special dinner.

Penny watched, looking worried, as Hollis walked determinedly to DiFazio's office.

He was peering at the screen over his keyboard, typing energetically.

DiFazio didn't look up, but said, "I can feel your vibe from here. I take it the penny lady told you that she saw me in your office."

"As a matter of fact, she did." Hollis dumped her coat and briefcase on one of the two chairs facing the desk and sat in the other. "Want to explain?"

He turned to face her. "I knew you were signing Mercer as a new client. I just wanted to show you how I could do more to assist you, especially now that you've got this high-profile criminal case."

"And how were you planning on showing me?"

DiFazio handed her a file of papers. "With this."

Hollis opened the folder, and her eyes grew wide as she flipped through the document.

"It's a draft of the Mercer Trust. It should be pretty close to final." He smiled. "I looked at your notes in the file, and I could tell how you were going to structure the trust. I couldn't figure out everything, but I did provide for the more tedious clauses and proposed several safety provisions."

Unsmiling, she reshuffled the pages and placed the file in her briefcase.

"Ever hear of attorney-client privilege?" Hollis said. "Lindsay Mercer has a complicated case. She hired me because she trusts me to keep her situation private."

She could tell that DiFazio was expecting a different response, probably one that showed her everlasting gratitude instead of her displeasure. Well, it wasn't going to happen.

He swallowed hard. "We both know that privilege obligation automatically extends to anyone on your legal team. I know I'm bound to confidentiality."

"But what you don't appear to know… Mr. DiFazio, is that *I* committed to draw up her trust and that *I* have a specific approach I wanted taken." She didn't try to hide her annoyance. "Please don't try to charge your hours worked on this document to this matter."

The color in Leo DiFazio's face had risen to the bright red Penny had described earlier. Hollis had a fleeting thought that he would never make a good criminal attorney with his feelings so evident. Still, she knew she'd probably overreacted—again. Even with a quick glance at his draft, she could tell he had saved her two or three hours of work tonight.

DiFazio stood and reached for his jacket hanging on the coat rack.

"I got in real early and I'm beat. I'm going home," he said, but he paused as he moved past her. "Sometimes you can be a difficult person to please."

She started to protest and then stopped. He was right.

A FEW HOURS LATER, at home, with promises of a fun-filled weekend, John had begged off to get some sleep. Hollis ate take-out, took a long bath, and finally, after a couple of hours, rubbed her eyes and closed her laptop. DiFazio had done a very good job. She didn't know why he set her off.

But he did.

SEVENTEEN

HOLLIS IGNORED THE smirk on Eleanor's face when she entered the lobby later than usual Monday morning.

"Hmm, John must be home," the receptionist said, pointedly looking at the clock. "Something kept you busy. It's almost seven thirty."

Hollis walked quickly past her. "Good morning, Eleanor. When Penny comes in, please ask her to see me."

"Of course," Eleanor said, obviously miffed.

Hollis opened her office and left the door ajar behind her. She looked out her window at the red lights of the backed-up traffic creeping onto the Bay Bridge. A small smile crept onto her face. Her morning had started with a playful John, who seemed reborn after his return to the field. He was chatty, confident, and loving. His mood was like the old days.

The old days.

Her "old" days were filled with self-doubt and humiliation. John had changed that considerably, but every so often she had flashbacks to her failed marriage and her subsequent decline, and unease would once again tighten her chest.

Hollis looked up to see Penny standing in her office doorway holding several folders. She nodded for her to come in.

"I think I've made an enemy of Leo," the paralegal said. "He's barely talking to me."

"He'll get over it. What have you got there?"

During the next hour, she prepared for her three o'clock appointment with Lindsay Mercer. She reviewed Penny's work and then concentrated on making finishing touches to the Mercer trust. Grudgingly, she had to admit that DiFazio's work had eased her load. The document was complete and copies were made. Hollis patted the top of the file.

"Lindsay Mercer is waiting for you in the small conference room," Eleanor announced on the intercom.

That was close.

Hollis entered the room to find her client staring out the window.

"I never get tired of looking at this view," Lindsay said without turning around.

"Neither do I. It's one of my main incentives for arriving early in the morning."

"So, let's get this done," Lindsay said, turning to take a seat. "I'm pleased you got the paperwork completed so quickly."

Hollis passed the small sheaf of pages. "Once you get past the…hmm…unique circumstances, it's a pretty standard trust. Your execution of the trust concludes my role until I'm notified of your…uh, your death."

Lindsay laughed.

She put on a pair of reading glasses and slowly read each page. Hollis watched her, and except for asking for a term clarification, Lindsay said little. Finally she came to the end and put her glasses away.

"This is good work. I noticed how you established your office as the contact for the trustee and the trustor. That way no one can locate Nina or my mother's whereabouts. Well, not without difficulty, anyway."

Hollis nodded. "I followed your request to establish a P.O. Box at the Oakland main post office. I'll check it periodically, and you can communicate with me that way. However, I will not know your location, and all terms of the trust will remain confidential. When the time comes, and your…death is confirmed, I'll file the certification with the court and distribute your estate to your cousin."

"You should have it in a few days. I think I'll have a heart attack—I'm under too much stress. I don't want to die from anything too messy." Lindsay gave a humorless laugh. She pointed to the document. "I take it I can sign now?"

"Yes, of course," Hollis said. "You'll sign in front of my assistant and she can notarize the document. I'll call for her."

Penny arrived and Hollis introduced the women. Within minutes, the trust was notarized and Penny had left.

Lindsay sighed deeply. "Well, I'll leave now. I have a flight tomorrow morning." Standing, she thrust out her hand for Hollis to shake.

"Goodbye, Hollis Morgan. It's not likely we will meet again."

"Goodbye, Lindsay Mercer. I wish you luck."

Hollis opened the door leading to the lobby, and as she did so, she uttered a soft gasp of surprise. Leo DiFazio stood there looking equally startled.

"I didn't know anyone was using the conference room," he said, peering around Hollis at Lindsay Mercer, who had turned her head away. He gave her a wide grin. "Hello, I'm an associate of Hollis's, Leo DiFazio."

Hollis looked up at the ceiling in irritation. She was

about to introduce Lindsay when the woman nodded slightly and stepped past her, ignoring DiFazio's outstretched hand.

"Hello. I'll leave you two to discuss work," Lindsay said over her shoulder as she walked down the hallway.

Hollis and Leo watched her make her way to the elevator.

"Was that Lindsay Mercer?" DiFazio asked.

"Yes, why?"

"I was curious to meet her after I did the work on her trust."

"Okay, well, you've met her." She faced him. "Uh, by the way, you did a good job with the final draft. I only had to make a few changes. It was a big help."

Faking shock, he stumbled into the wall. "Where's my calendar? I got a word of praise from Ms. Morgan." He jutted his chin toward the departing client. "Where's she off to?"

"If anyone asks you," Hollis said, "tell them you don't know."

WHEN SHE GOT HOME, John was sitting on a kitchen stool, bent over the newspaper spread out on the counter. He had a glass of red wine close by.

"Hi." She gave him a deep kiss. "I like coming home to you."

"Coming home is the best part of leaving," he murmured against her neck.

"Sorry about dinner. We didn't talk much last night," she said, recalling that talk had not been on the agenda. But now she stepped back and peered at him. "How was it? Did the assignment go the way it was supposed to?"

"It went very well." He put his arm around her waist.

"It felt good working with a team again." He nodded toward the living room. "Come on, let's sit down and share a glass of wine. Lately we've only said hi in passing as we rushed out the door. I want to hear about your work."

"Hey, it's not like I really hear about yours." Hollis nudged him.

She examined him closely for any signs of tiredness. To her relief, he looked elated and peaceful at the same time. Taking the bottle of wine with them, they moved to the sofa in front of the unlit fireplace.

Hollis laughed. "Don't think I didn't notice the general single-sentence avoidance description you gave about your work—but I understand the need for secrecy." She snuggled next to him. "Me? My two top clients have completely different concerns, but they are ironically similar in how they approach their issues."

"How's that criminal case? Is Vince helping?"

"Yes, he is. I think he's trying to bond with the client first. We'll see. I just introduced them." She tapped him on the chest. "But the real news is that Vince is in love. She seems to be a nice young woman."

Her thoughts drifted to her conversation with Vince.

"What's that look for?" John asked.

"Nothing, I was just remembering us." She grinned and took a sip of wine. "But back to the cases… I can tell you that my client is a better liar than I am. And he's immature enough to think that he can control the situation by withholding the truth, and even worse, withholding evidence."

"Hmm, sounds like Vince will have his heart and his hands full." John looked thoughtful. "But he can handle himself. He's perceptive, and I don't think your client will be able to get away with much."

"I hope so," she said. "My other client is in the witness protection program. I'm her trustee. My work with her is…complicated, and I don't think she's telling me everything either."

John ran his fingers through her hair. "You've heard the saying, 'Like attracts like,' haven't you?"

Hollis playfully punched him in the arm. "What's that supposed to mean?"

"I'm jus' sayin', that's all. Jus' sayin'."

EIGHTEEN

AFTER FINALIZING CLIENT documents and checking Di-Fazio's work, Hollis put aside her probate practice and prepared for her meeting with Justin.

Vince had dropped him off in the lobby and sullenly reported he was going to check in on the mailroom. He was clearly still upset with her.

They always shoot the messenger.

Now, she and Justin were sitting in her office, where they'd been for the past hour. She could hear staff chatting in the hallway, even the ding of the elevator, but the young man in front of her was uncommunicative and apparently unwilling to focus on his situation.

Hollis waited for him to respond to her question.

"We will stay here as long as it takes, Justin," she said in a patient tone. "I want to know what else was in that Nike bag."

"Can I have some water?"

"No, you already had two bottles. Next you'll be asking to go to the bathroom. You're stalling."

"I'm thirsty, that's all," he said with a pout. "I'm supposed to get together with Vince and hang out."

Hollis shrugged. "He'll wait until we're finished here," she said. "Justin, I don't think you really understand your circumstances." She tapped the file between them. "You are not free. You're still charged. You are *arrested* and out on bail."

"But—"

"There are no 'buts.' Unless you deliver the goods, either by the crooks revealing themselves—with you as bait, I might add—or give the DA whatever it is they're looking for, you're going to be very unhappy. If you don't stop playing as if this were a game, you will wind up back in jail, or *dead*."

The word hung between them as if blasted over a loudspeaker. He squirmed and his face turned red. He pressed the heel of his hand to his forehead.

"You don't get it: what I have doesn't matter," he said, looking her in the eyes. "I'm a dead man either way. I want to enjoy the time I have now. They're going to get me whether I'm outside or in."

Hollis was taken aback by his matter-of-fact words.

"Justin, that's not true. The DA will lock them up and…."

He sniffed, his lips curling into a smirk.

"They want what I found in the bag, and if I tell you where it is…." He paused, then continued, "If I tell you, then you're as dead as me."

"I'm willing to take my chances."

He looked at her and shook his head. His eyes watered as if the reality of his situation and future was staring him in the face. He slowly shook his head.

"I can't tell you, and I won't." For emphasis he crossed his arms over his chest.

Hollis raised her eyes to the ceiling.

Justin started to speak, then pursed his lips and shook his head.

THOUGH PRODDED FURTHER, Justin refused to give up any information that Hollis could use to lead to his release or the capture of the people who threatened him. She finally summoned Vince from the mailroom to say Justin was ready to be returned to his family. When he arrived at her office a few minutes later, she detected no hint of their earlier disagreement other than a slight coolness in his manner.

She beckoned him into the hallway. "Talk to Justin. See if he'll confide in you. We need to know what was on that data stick and get him to stop playing television drama."

Vince nodded. "I'll get him to tell me. He's not really a bad dude."

He reached to open the door.

"Uh, Vince," she began, "about the other...."

He turned to face her. A smile played on his lips. "Don't worry, we're good. I know you were trying to help."

They went back into her office, and Justin jumped up from his seat once more, again like a puppy eager to play in the park.

Hollis shook her head in frustration. "All right, Justin, let's meet later this week to touch base and see how things are working out."

"Don't worry, Hollis. I'll think about what you said," he said over his shoulder.

She knew he had no intention of doing any such thing.

NINETEEN

"HOLLIS." PENNY ENTERED the office. "I hate to bother you with…with everything that's going on with the Eastland case. But I took a strange call from the County Recorder's office."

"County Recorder?" She swiveled to face the paralegal. "What about?"

"She wanted to speak directly with you, but I didn't see any reason why I couldn't help her." Penny didn't try to hide her indignation. "She insisted that she could only speak with you. So, I told her that was not going to happen, and if she wanted you to get a message, she was going to have to leave it with me."

"And…?"

"Snooty clerk." Penny stepped up to Hollis's desk. "Well, she thought about it a moment and finally got it out."

"If only *you* would get it out." Hollis's level of irritation was rising. "You came in here to tell me, so tell me. What did the Recorder want?"

"There was a note that said to contact you when the certificate was ready for processing."

"Certificate?"

Penny raised her eyebrows. "Yes, Lindsay Mercer's death certificate."

Hollis stared blankly for a moment.

She worked fast.

"Thanks, Penny, I'll… I'll follow up," Hollis said. "Ah…she knew she was dying and it was just a matter of days."

Penny gave a quick snort. "Well, she certainly looked healthy on Monday. What was wrong with her?"

Hollis shrugged. "She didn't say, and I didn't want to invade her privacy," she said curtly. She reached behind her for a folder and handed it to the woman. "Here's her file. You can start processing it. I have to check on something else at the courthouse, so I'll pick up the death certificate on my way home."

"Okay," Penny replied, "but what's the rush?"

"No rush," Hollis insisted. "Let's just not drag it out. I'm dealing with this Eastland case, and I have to go to the courthouse anyway." She looked at her calendar. "Oh, and book me the firm's car for my drive to Ahwahnee first thing next week. I'll want to get there and back."

Penny nodded. "You sure you don't want to spend the night?"

"Only if I have to, and I shouldn't have to."

Hollis lied easily. The fewer people who knew about the supposed death of Lindsay Mercer, the better. She smiled. She was doing her part. Hopefully, Ms. Mercer had taken care of the rest.

HOLLIS STARED AT the piece of paper in her hand. Something was terribly wrong.

She tapped on the counter of the County Recorder to catch the attention of the young girl chatting with her office mate.

She cleared her throat. "Excuse me, I have another question."

With a backwards glance to her friend, the girl approached the counter. "Yes, what's the matter?"

"This death certificate is incorrect. Who can I talk to about getting a corrected one?"

"I'm sorry. You're saying that the name is incorrect or...."

"No, the name is fine. Lindsay Mercer is dead, but she didn't die like this."

"This came from the coroner's office, see." She pointed to a line. "And that's the doctor who signed the death certificate, so she *did* die like that. I'm sorry."

Hollis shook her head. "No, she didn't. Lindsay Mercer was supposed to... I mean, I thought the cause of death was a heart attack."

The girl read upside down. "Well, according to this, she died of a gunshot wound to the back."

TWENTY

On Thursday Morning, Hollis sat in her office, staring at the certificate.

Shot in the chest!

Was this Lindsay's idea of a macabre joke? Or did someone discover her identity and whereabouts—and here was her worst fear—*really* kill her? She glanced at the time. It was almost four o'clock. She was waiting for nine o'clock to call Doctor Aaron Lamb, the doctor who signed Lindsay's death certificate. The doctor's offices were in Walnut Creek. Hollis had googled him and discovered that, in addition to his work for the county, he had a private practice and worked out of Crestview Hospital in the trendy city's downtown district.

She took out her phone and punched in a number.

"Stephanie, it's me."

"Hollis, you okay? You sound funny."

"Meet me outside your building in the parking lot in ten minutes. Do you have a few minutes to talk?"

"Business or pleasure?"

"Business, definitely."

"Meet me in the lobby. I'll be there in five minutes."

Stephanie was true to her word. Hollis had just sat down when her friend appeared. They found distant seats away from the elevator in the lounge area.

"I need you to look into something for me," Hollis said. "I can't go into the full story right now, but I need your help to follow up on a death certificate. I want to verify the cause of death and the deceased."

"I thought you were kidding about coming up with something to distract me from Dan, because it's not necessary. I really have a lot to do."

"I'm not kidding."

She handed her the death certificate.

Stephanie gazed at the paper and grimaced. "You're not making any sense. What's questionable about the death certificate? I know Dr. Lamb—he's legit." She handed the paper back. "What's your concern? Is the person still alive? Or do you think the cause of death is incorrect?"

"Both."

Stephanie just stared at her in disbelief.

"Maybe you could give me the short version."

Hollis took the next few minutes to provide background, withholding Lindsay Mercer's personal details and her criminal activities. Stephanie's need to know was best kept limited.

"So, you think she's still alive?"

"Look, I wouldn't be talking to you if I thought she was still alive. She's *supposed* to be still alive," Hollis muttered, "but a gunshot to the chest was not the way she planned to go."

"Witness Protection Program…interesting," Stephanie mused. "This is the first time I've encountered a participant."

"You still haven't encountered one. I don't want you involved with this. I just need you to verify that the cause of Lindsay Mercer's death was a gunshot wound."

Stephanie wrinkled her forehead. "Well, I guess my first stop would be the morgue. According to procedure, they would be waiting to hear from her family or friends to decide what to do with the body." She pursed her lips. "On the other hand, since it's a violent crime, it might come to my department anyway."

"That's right," Hollis agreed, and then paused, remembering that there was nothing procedural about this matter. "On the other hand, it's more likely the DA has taken over."

"No more speculation." Stephanie stood. "Let me get back to my lab. I'll check into things and let you know."

She headed for the elevator and then turned to catch Hollis's eye.

"Thanks, Hollis."

"For what?"

"For giving me something else to work through besides my sad story."

"Steph, I didn't make this up. This is for real."

"I know." She smiled. "Thanks, anyway."

IT WAS CLOSE to lunchtime when Hollis returned to the firm. She checked the board to verify that Gordon was in and behind the closed door. She tapped lightly, then poked her head in. He was on the phone, but he waved at her to take a seat.

Pretending not to know that he was on a personal call, she carefully read and reread her notes.

Within minutes, he ended the conversation.

"My forty-two-year-old sister," Gordon said, clicking off the phone. "She went back to college for a degree in art history. Now she wants me to help pay down her student loans by giving her a loan of my own."

Hollis gave him a quick smile. "I imagine you're an easier lender than a bank."

"Yeah, well, tell that to my ex-wife." He tapped his fingers on his desk. "Well, enough about me. What's going on? Did you get the bag contents from Eastland? We can't let the clock run out on discovery."

She shook her head. "We have three weeks before the discovery deadline." She crossed her arms. "This is something else. Remember my probate client, Lindsay Mercer, well—"

Gordon's phone trilled and he glanced down at the screen.

He put the phone down. "I'll call them back. What is it?"

"I just picked up Lindsay Mercer's death certificate."

"Hmm, she didn't waste any time."

"No, she didn't," Hollis said. "But the bothersome part is that she told me she would arrange for a death by heart attack in some large city, maybe in another state. She wanted no mess and little attention."

"Yeah?"

"Well, according to the certificate, she was shot in the chest in San Lucian."

Gordon's focus was on her, but she knew him well enough to realize that he wasn't looking at her so much as processing the situation.

"Unfortunately," he said, "there are so many variables in this case that it's best to move cautiously until all the players appear. Find out what's going on. Just keep me in the loop," he picked up his phone, "and don't get into trouble."

DR. LAMB'S RECEPTIONIST was sneaking looks at Hollis from over her counter. A couple of times, Hollis caught her, and the young woman blushed. There was no one else in the waiting room. She'd called from the firm, and after explaining repeatedly why she had to see the doctor that day, she convinced the woman to allow her to confer with Dr. Lamb. He'd given her a time and agreed to "squeeze her in."

Hollis glanced at the clock over the desk.

"Do you expect Dr. Lamb to return soon?" she asked.

"Oh, he's here." The girl smiled. "He has someone in his office."

Hollis frowned. "Does he know I'm here?"

For the almost thirty minutes she'd been waiting, unless there was a secret button, the young girl had never left her desk or picked up a phone.

"I'm pretty sure he does." The girl grinned and pointed to a small camera positioned in the corner of the ceiling over her desk. "It's for after-hours when this desk isn't covered. He can see what patients are here and how many."

Hollis pressed her lips together and tried to suppress the impatience rising in her chest. After all, he had made room in his schedule. Turning to her briefcase, she lifted out her iPad. If she were in for a wait, she could use the time to do some work. Evidently, that did the trick, because before she could finish entering her passcode, Lamb came to the door.

"Ms. Morgan, sorry to keep you waiting," he said in a sonorous voice. "I can see you now."

His office was stark and devoid of color—a monotone beige throughout. A simple desk of light maple and two tan chairs stood in the middle of the room, with four half-filled blond-wood bookcases hugging the wall behind. Even the book covers seemed tan and light beige. There were two other doors besides the one

Hollis walked through. One presumably led to his examination room; the other she guessed allowed his patients to depart unseen. He caught her glance.

"For patient privacy," he said. "Now, what do you want to know about Lindsay Mercer's death?"

He sat behind his desk and she faced him with what she hoped was an engaging smile.

"Dr. Lamb, as I told you, I'm the attorney for the estate of Lindsay Mercer." Hollis handed him her card. "She confided in me about…about her ongoing health concerns."

Hollis cleared her throat. She had practiced what she was going to say, hoping to get as much as she could out of Lamb without giving up any information of her own. "Her violent death came as a…a shock. I just found out this morning that she had died. I'm going to meet with the DA's office next, but your name was on the certificate. Can you tell me the particulars of the injury? Were you her regular doctor?"

Lamb put glasses on. "No, I'm not her regular physician, and I have no idea who that is. I'm sure if you're going to be meeting with the police, they will know, or will want to know what you know." He looked down at the open file in front of him and read, "'Two days ago, I was on duty at Crestview Hospital when a white female, estimated to be in her late-thirties or early forties, was brought in through emergency with a gunshot wound to her back. I removed a 9mm bullet that had lodged in her back. The bullet had pierced her aorta, and she had profuse internal bleeding. Standard life-saving measures were utilized, but none were effective, and eighteen minutes after admission, Mercer was pronounced dead. As physician on duty, I signed the death certificate.'"

Hollis had perfected the art of reading upside down, and she noted that there were two pages of single-spaced typed text in addition to the hospital regulation form from which the doctor had read. The pages were on pale-blue stationery.

"So, to be clear, you actually had a body that was identified as Lindsay Mercer?"

He frowned. "Well, of course there was an actual body. And there was no reason to question the identification provided by the sheriff's office."

"Did you notice any other signs of a physical condition?"

"No." He bristled. "What do you mean?"

"When I spoke with Lindsay Mercer, she mentioned a cancerous condition. I wondered if you saw any evidence of that—perhaps radiation burns?"

He waved at the air. "No, I didn't." He closed the file. "Is there anything else, Ms. Morgan? I've been up since five a.m., and I still have patients to see and surgery in the morning."

"Oh, you're a surgeon?"

He squinted. "Why? Is that an issue?"

She gathered her purse and briefcase. "I was wondering why a private doctor, excuse me, a private surgeon would be working in a county hospital emergency room."

"They're always short of staff, and I... I volunteer. It's my way of giving back."

"Of course," she said, heading for the door. "Goodbye, Doctor."

"SORRY TO KEEP bothering you, Hollis," Penny said from the doorway. "I confirmed your car reservation. I'll have it brought to the garage on Sunday evening, and you can leave whenever you want on Monday. I told them to make the return for the next day, just in case."

"Thanks, Penny," Hollis said. "One more thing… make sure you run a GPS hardcopy for me. Nina Shaw lives in a little town near Yosemite, and I don't want to be wandering around because my car doesn't have the latest mapping update."

"Consider it done."

Hollis punched in a number on her desk phone.

"Mrs. Powell, I left an earlier message," she said into the voicemail system. "It's very important that you contact me as soon as possible." She left her name and contact number again, and clicked off.

She looked out her window, lost in thought. Gloria Powell could be anywhere. Lindsay Mercer had said that her mother worked, but she didn't say where. The woman could be on vacation, or at a conference. The answering machine reinforced that Hollis had the right number; Lindsay's voice was similar to her mother's. But it was more than frustrating not to be able to contact her.

This was a job for Penny. She hit the speed dial on her phone.

"Penny, I'm glad I caught you," said Hollis. "I need you to get in contact with Lindsay Mercer's mother, a Gloria Powell, age approximately sixty, living in Indiana. Here's her phone number. I need to talk with her."

"How soon?"

"Yesterday would be great," she said. "But tomorrow morning would be good."

"All right, I'll find her," Penny replied. "Oh, Vince checked in and said to tell you that Justin Eastland was behaving himself, and that they planned to see you tomorrow. I hope it's okay, but I made a lunch reservation for the three of you."

"You did the right thing. I'm not sure these are 'reservation' type guys, but it's fine."

Penny left, and just as Hollis reached for her phone, it chimed.

"I hope you're sitting down," Stephanie said breathlessly.

Hollis grabbed a pad and pen. "Okay, what did you find out?"

"That's a real body in the morgue, and judging by the identification you gave me, it's your client, Lindsay Mercer."

HOLLIS SAT IN the single guest chair in Penny's office, dismayed as well as thoughtful. She needed to mull things over, but after getting an urgent request to stop by, found herself in the paralegal's work space.

"What is it that you wanted to see me about?" she asked.

She noticed that Penny, in her own way, was attempting to build to a dramatic reveal. She clasped her hands and leaned across her desk.

"Well, I couldn't make your impossible time-traveling goal of yesterday, but I found Gloria Powell. She's living here…in California."

Hollis did a double-take. "What?"

"I know," Penny nodded, "I can't believe it either. But I have one more thing to verify, and if I'm right, Gloria lives in Albany."

"Wait… New York?"

"No, I said California." Penny glanced down at her

print-out. "It appears that after Lindsay was put in the program and left, Gloria moved around quite a bit. She sold her house in Indiana and moved to Ohio. She has a sister who lives there. After living with her sister for about six months, she moved to Denver. She worked in a real estate office and lived there for about eighteen months. Then about three months ago, she rented a condo in Albany, and that's where I think she is."

"How were you able to locate her?"

"The first piece of the puzzle was the hardest. Lindsay left you with her name and small bits of information about where she lived, but not where she was. So, I ran her through PeopleSearch, the public records database. I found eight Gloria Powells with possible matching backgrounds, then ran each one down."

Hollis looked at her in disbelief. "My goodness, Penny, that must have taken hours."

"Well, we wouldn't be having this conversation if I hadn't hit pay dirt," Penny said in her matter-of-fact way. "It was a bit mundane, but I was prepared to widen my circle of inquiry if necessary."

"Of course, you would have." Hollis smiled. "You are an analyst supreme."

Penny rarely smiled, and she didn't now. Except that Hollis noticed a flush of color on her cheeks.

"So, she was making her way across the country, maybe to be near her daughter," Hollis mused. "Despite what Lindsay told me, she was keeping in contact with her family." She leaned back in the chair. "What's the last piece you have to verify?"

Penny, now back in familiar and unemotional territory, cleared her throat. "I'm pretty sure that she lives in the same neighborhood as Mark and Rena Haddon."

HOLLIS LOOKED AROUND Mark's office in admiration. It was large, with an anteroom containing a walnut conference table and chairs. In the center was a massive executive desk, and in front of that was a small sofa and an adjacent coffee table. The view through the Golden Gate Bridge to the Pacific Ocean was jaw-dropping and worthy of a junior partner in the world's fifth largest law firm.

She smiled; he had done well for himself.

"What's that for?" Mark said, bringing her a cup of tea and a napkin.

"What?"

"The smile. What were you thinking about?"

"Copy machines," she replied, taking a sip of tea.

He gave her a puzzled look and then broke into a hearty laugh. "You mean the first time we met each other. Yeah, I've come a long way." He looked around his office. "And you know, I still don't know how to clear jammed pages."

Hollis grinned. "Well, at least now you don't need to."

"No, no, I don't." He gave her a long look. "Okay, enough of the easy conversation. You told my secretary it was critical. What's wrong?"

Hollis put her cup down. "Mark, this isn't easy, but Lindsay Mercer might be really dead."

"Dead?" His voice rose. "What do you mean, *might* be?"

She took a deep breath, and in the next minutes explained the recent happenings, ending with Hollis's suspicions about Lindsay Mercer's body in the morgue.

"Mark, I had Stephanie check it out, and she confirmed the death certificate is correct. The body is Lindsay's." Hollis paused. "But while I didn't know her well, Lindsay clearly stated that she would have a heart attack." She stared out the window. "I'd like to get her mother to provide a final identification. Maybe you could take me with you to meet her."

Her words hung in the air.

"Oh. You know." Mark held up his hand. "Before you get bent out of shape, Lindsay said she wanted to tell you her story personally. Her mother was tangential to the larger issue of her staying under the radar."

"She's not tangential anymore. She's front and center. Her daughter's body is in the morgue. I'll ask… why didn't you tell me that her mother was here, and that you knew her?"

"I should have." Mark rubbed the back of his neck. "But Lindsay's paranoia won me over. I can't believe she's really dead." He took a deep breath. "She was adamant that no one should know the connection between the two of them. Evidently Gloria Powell moved out here on her own a few months ago without telling her daughter. Lindsay had called her, and Gloria used caller ID to call back. She would make a pretty good detective. From that call, she found out that Lindsay was in the Bay Area and followed her here. Lindsay refused to see her. For several weeks, I was the go-between, passing small amounts of money from Lindsay to her mother. I never saw them together." He fidgeted with a paperclip, but when he spoke, his voice was low and somber, "And until you just told me, I never knew about Lindsay's participation in criminal activity or her deceased husband and child."

"She was extremely secretive." Hollis sighed. "I've been in her position, feeling the need to protect my past. Trust wasn't in my vocabulary. I can completely understand her being defensive and suspicious of everyone."

"At first," Mark said, "she was angry when she discovered that Gloria had tracked her down. I think that's when she got the idea to disappear again. If her mother could find her, it wouldn't take long for a professional. Having her mother nearby saved her from worry, but I'm surprised she didn't feel comfortable telling me the rest."

"I don't think she wanted you to think less of her. You mattered to her."

"Me *and* Rena," he said. "She helped us decorate our home. She even watched Christopher for us once." He threw his head back as if willing the tension in his neck to disappear. "I think I should be the one to tell Mrs. Powell that her daughter may be dead."

"Maybe we both should," Hollis said. "It might help if I'm there to tell her about Lindsay's last wishes. I just wish I knew how much she told her mother."

Mark waved away her concern. "Gloria would have wanted to know everything. She seems to be a strong woman and was reconciled to her daughter's way of life."

Hollis shook her head. "I had no idea until Penny told me this morning that Gloria Powell was even in the area. Lindsay withheld that little piece of information from me, as well." She frowned. "But, yes, I think we should both pay her a visit and see if Mrs. Powell is willing to accompany us to the morgue. Even though the cause of death is unexpected, I have no choice but to process Lindsay's trust as she authorized. I'm scheduled to see Nina Shaw on Thursday."

"Today is done and I've got a late meeting out of the office." He glanced at his calendar. "I'll contact Gloria and tell her you're coming with me to see her. If she agrees, I'll meet you there tomorrow morning at nine. We'll broach the subject of the morgue visit with her then."

He scribbled an address and phone number on a piece of paper.

JOHN WAS SITTING on the deck with a glass of wine in his hand, staring out over the backyard. Hollis came up to him and gave him a kiss on the cheek, and when he held his head up to hers, their next kiss was full on the lips. Still not speaking, she went back into the kitchen and brought back her own wine glass. She took a seat in the chair next to his.

"Any ideas for dinner that don't involve using our kitchen?" she said.

He chuckled. "I'm for going out, or taking in. What about a pizza?"

"We had pizza day before yesterday. I think you would eat pizza every day if you could." Hollis grinned.

He pretended to ponder her words. "You're right." He took a sip from his glass. "But I'm not hungry for anything much."

She frowned. "What's the matter? You're always hungry."

"Will you do me a favor?" he snapped. "Stop evaluating my responses as if I'm on the brink of a medical emergency."

"John, I'm just tired. I had a tough day and—"

"I'm sorry, I didn't mean that." He bent toward her with his elbows on his thighs, his hands clutched under his chin. "In light of what I just said, you're going to realize what a hypocrite I can be. I have a special favor to ask of you."

"What?"

He took her hand. "You're working on two potentially sensitive cases. I have to go away this Friday for a week, maybe ten days. It's a…a follow-up to my last assignment. I don't want to be worried about you. I want you to promise me that you won't do anything stupid until I return."

Hollis knew what he wasn't saying. He could make mistakes if he was concerned about her well-being.

She took back her hand from his. "Your definition of stupid, or mine?"

"My definition."

For a long moment, they looked into each other's eyes.

Hollis turned away. "You are a huge hypocrite. Where are you going?"

John sighed. "I can't tell you."

She wrinkled her brow. "Can you tell me if you're in the U.S. or another country?"

"I can't tell you."

"I'll only think the worst," she protested then, realizing her ploy to manipulate his guilt was not getting her anywhere. She took a sip of wine. "All right, if you promise not to take unnecessary risks, I won't do anything stupid until you get back."

TWENTY-ONE

THE TOWERS IN Albany consisted of a group of high-rise condominiums on the edge of Highway 80 as it curved around the East San Francisco Bay. Located between Berkeley and Oakland, the complex had risen from the muck of a superfund toxic site to become one of the priciest communities in the area. Gloria Powell's condo didn't face the water but had a panoramic view of the Berkeley Hills.

Mark had texted that he was running a little late but for Hollis to go ahead and introduce herself. The doorbell had barely finished chiming before the door was snatched open.

"You must be Hollis," the woman said, putting out her hand and drawing Hollis in. "Mark called to say he would be late and that you would get here first. What he didn't say was why you two were here at all."

Lindsay's mother was tall, nearly six feet. She had dark hair and thick Frieda Kahlo eyebrows. Her dark eyes penetrated like an X-ray. The piercing eyes combined with the small rosebud mouth and patrician nose made it a face one was unlikely to forget. She had to be in her sixties, but she looked twenty years younger. Hollis could see the resemblance to her daughter.

"Mrs. Powell, Mark should be here any minute," Hollis said. "I'm an attorney as well. Your daughter retained me as her probate attorney and—"

"Call me Gloria," she insisted. "Probate? Is Lindsay all right?"

The intercom buzzer went off. Hollis sighed with relief.

"That must be Mark," Gloria said, jumping up to let him in. "He's a very nice man. Lindsay told me I could trust him. This is about her, isn't it?"

The distraction of Mark's arrival saved Hollis from having to answer.

When he entered the room, he exchanged looks with Hollis, and from the nearly imperceptible shake of her head, understood that she had not told the woman about her daughter.

"Gloria, it's good to see you again." He gave her a hug. "I see you've met Hollis. You're probably wondering why we're here."

"No, not really. It's about Lindsay." It was a statement, not a question. Her face was now somber with no hint of its former smile. She looked from one to the other. "She's dead, isn't she?"

Mark sat next to her and took her hand without answering. "We may need your help. I recommended Hollis to Lindsay to help her write her trust. Lindsay already confided to Hollis about the witness protection program and her…circumstances."

Gloria turned to look at Hollis, who nodded.

Mark went on, "Lindsay told her that she was planning another disappearance and that Hollis should invoke its terms on presentation of her death certificate." He put an arm around Gloria's shoulders. "This is where it gets tough."

Gloria paled, but gestured for him to continue.

"Lindsay told Hollis she would fake a heart attack, likely in another state, but when Hollis got the certificate, it had the cause of death as a gunshot, here in California."

Gloria inhaled sharply and clapped a hand to her mouth.

Hollis edged forward. "I met your daughter a few times, Mrs. Powell. And the authorities are definitely holding a deceased person who appears to have Lindsay's identification. I know that Lindsay was planning on arranging her…new life, and this could be part of the plan, but—"

"You want me to go to the morgue?"

Mark sighed. "Yes."

There was a silence that Hollis thought would never end, even though probably less than a minute passed.

"I've been to the morgue before." Gloria put her hands over her eyes. "When Lindsey first went into the program, her manager kept discovering her location. One time the police thought he'd been successful. They asked me to identify the body." She paused. "But it wasn't her." She looked up. "Maybe…maybe it won't be her this time either."

"Maybe not," Hollis said quietly.

"Give me a couple of minutes. I'll get my coat."

The woman was aging before Hollis's very eyes. While Gloria Powell had not shed a tear, she appeared to have lost hope. As she rose to retrieve her coat, her shoulders seemed to sag with the weight of the world.

When she was out of the room, Hollis quickly took out her cellphone and looked over at Mark. "I need to set things up at the morgue with Gil Tunney in the DA's office."

"I've never been to the morgue," he said thoughtfully.

"Neither have I."

THE RUSSELL COUNTY MORGUE was wedged between Alameda and Russell Counties. Thanks to an early land purchase by the government and unrealized prosperity, the site was in the middle of nowhere, waiting for the economy to reach it. According to Wikipedia, it was a single-story building shaped like a squared-off infinity sign. One end held the examining rooms, lab, and refrigeration unit, the other held administrative offices, files, and the car pool.

The drive to the morgue was quiet. Mark drove, and Hollis suggested that the long-legged Mrs. Powell would be more comfortable in the front. From time to time, the elderly woman would break the silence by recalling episodes from Lindsay's childhood, when their entire family was together.

In a quiet moment, Hollis leaned toward the front seat. "Mrs. Powell, what did Lindsay say when she discovered you knew where she'd been relocated? Wasn't that dangerous? I mean, weren't you concerned that her enemies would be on the lookout to see if you would lead them to her?"

"At first, yes, I was worried," Gloria Powell replied in a choked voice. "But I couldn't stand not knowing if she was okay or not. We talked it through, and she said it wouldn't matter anymore. She had a plan that was foolproof. She wanted us to be together; she wanted to take care of me." She shook her head. "She was the one who was diagnosed with cancer, and she wanted to take care of *me*."

Hollis sat back and exchanged looks with Mark in the mirror. "I'm sorry."

"I hadn't heard from her. She was going to call me this Sunday." Looking out the window, Powell continued, "If Lindsay is...gone now, all I have left is Nina, a niece, my sister's daughter."

"Oh, Mrs. Powell," Hollis said. "I'm planning on driving to Ahwahnee to meet your niece, Nina Shaw. And... Lindsay told me about her plan. She wanted me to make sure you'd be provided for in the event she...well, she knew that she could trust Nina. Over the phone, she seems like a nice person."

Gloria Powell looked out the side window. "Nina's a good woman," she murmured. "She's led a troubled life, but she's turning it around. My sister died some years ago in a car accident. Nina was distraught, but she's held it together. If Lindsay's gone now, there's just the two of us."

They pulled into a space in the less than half-full parking lot. It was a cool, foggy morning. An ambulance, with its doors wide open, was unloading a gurney at the far end of the building.

While waiting for Gloria, Hollis had called Gordon to update him on the latest developments and the trip to the morgue.

"Don't even bother going to the waiting room," he said. "The room is named appropriately. Nobody is in a hurry, and you'll wait there for an hour before a clerk appears. Instead, go straight to the 'Administrative Staff Only' door. They're all in there. They don't want anybody to see that they're doing absolutely nothing, so you'll get served fast."

She had Mark and Gloria wait in the entry, and she did as he suggested. After confirming that the chair behind the reception desk was vacant, and after glancing at the people sitting restlessly in the plastic chairs—a couple and a well-dressed man—she went through the administrative staff door.

"Can I help you?"

Hollis looked around. The room was full of desks. Two facing rows of desks formed a wide aisle leading to large double doors. Men and women were busily tapping away on computers or talking amongst themselves.

"I'm here with some people to see Assistant DA Tunney. My name is Hollis Morgan. He asked me to meet him here."

The young woman, dressed in jeans, white blouse, and navy-blue jacket, tapped a few keys and checked her computer screen.

"Not here, honey," she said. "You need to go to the other side of the complex. He's probably waiting for you at Gate Two in the receiving complex." She gestured with her head toward the double doors.

They left the offices and strode outside along a cement walkway that rose and fell like a ribbon over the path to the receiving complex. After they turned a corner, Hollis spotted Tunney talking with a police officer. Beside them, an older man wearing a white lab coat was shaking his head and pointing over his shoulder. They approached when Tunney waved them forward.

Hollis made brief introductions. It was clear that everyone wanted to get the viewing over with.

"Mrs. Powell, we've been trying to get in touch with

you in Denver," Tunney said. "It's good that you're here. We would appreciate it if you gave your contact information to my officer."

"Of course," Gloria said curtly.

Tunney moved them to the entry. "This is Dr. Fell and Officer Williams, both of whom are assigned to Lindsay Mercer's case. Detective Cook contacted me, Ms. Morgan. He said you raised an issue with the cause of death."

Gloria swayed and Mark took her arm.

"Mr. Tunney," Hollis began, "if we could—"

He nodded vigorously. "Yes, well, because of the sensitivity of Ms. Mercer's…er, status, and the fact that her case was handled by the FBI and none of us have met her, it would be helpful, Mrs. Powell, to have your… your input."

Dr. Fell walked ahead to a ramp. "All right, then, let's go in." He pushed open the door, and the group walked into a long hallway with several closed-door offices on one side and a large open area with a glass-panel half wall on the other.

Fell unlocked one of the doors. They entered behind him.

"This is our autopsy lab," he said, moving steadily toward the rear of the room.

They followed his fast footsteps. Hollis kept her eyes straight ahead.

"This is the refrigeration room." He pointed and opened the door.

Hollis felt herself stiffen. She'd seen dead persons before, but never as many as were stored in the wall of closed stainless-steel drawers. Or the six covered bodies on gurneys along the wall. She shivered, but it had little to do with the cold.

"Over here, Gil." Fell moved to the closest table of the three lined up along the wall. "This is our Lindsay Mercer." He pulled back the sheet to the shoulders. "Mrs. Powell, can you confirm that this is your daughter? We want to make sure of the identity."

Mark guided Gloria by the arm to the table.

Hollis followed closely behind, her eyes averted until she stood next to them, and then she opened them wide.

Mrs. Powell leaned over the figure and gasped, her hand covering her mouth. She stepped back and bumped into Hollis.

"Oh, I'm sorry," she cried, "but that's not Lindsay. That's not my daughter; that's my niece, Nina."

"What!" Hollis blurted out.

"Your niece?" Mark and Tunney said together.

"That is not Lindsay." Gloria Powell returned to look at the body. She leaned over and started to sob. "I'm sorry, my nerves. I thought… I thought it would be Lindsay." She accepted a tissue from a box Dr. Fell handed her. "How did Nina die?"

Fell cleared his throat. "I'm very sorry, Mrs. Powell. Your niece died from a gunshot wound to the back. Did she have enemies?"

"Do you mean who would want to kill her?" Gloria said, her voice regaining its strength. "She was murdered. I don't know… I mean, I didn't know Nina that well anymore."

"Are you sure, Mrs. Powell?" Clearly frustrated, Tunney shook his head. "Then why was she carrying your daughter's identification?" He looked around.

"Perhaps we can move this…meeting to another space." He pointed in the direction of the door.

Fell nodded. "Yes, of course. We can meet in my office."

He led the way out into the hallway, clearly as disturbed by the revelation as they all were.

Fell's office was a glass-enclosed area within the larger open space. It contained a long narrow table covered with stacks of folders and loose papers. He hurried to wheel in more chairs.

"It's getting late," Tunney said, taking the chair closest to the front of the room. "But we need to get a few things settled while we're all here."

"I'm so glad my sister can't see this," Gloria murmured, dazed. "I guess I need to arrange for Nina's burial."

Mark put his arm around the woman's shoulders.

Fell squirmed in his chair. "This is going to take a while to straighten out. If I could just report on what I know.… I need to leave in about fifteen minutes. It's my anniversary, and I promised—"

"Fine," Tunney interrupted. "Then we'll hear from you first, and the rest of us will reconvene in my office first thing in the morning."

He looked around at everyone, as if daring to hear another objection. The room was silent.

"Good. Now, Dr. Fell, is there anything you've discovered about the…deceased?" He nodded to Gloria Powell. "Excuse me, I mean Ms. Shaw."

Fell shook his head. "No, it appears the vic…uh, Ms. Shaw, was right-handed. There is more muscle attachment on the dominant side. Then there was GSR—that is, gunshot residue—on her hands and clothing. The position of the wound indicates the deceased was shot in the back," he continued in a rush, not looking at Gloria. "It was clearly a violent crime. My assistant is conducting a full autopsy and toxicology report tonight, and you should have results before noon tomorrow."

Tunney turned to Gloria Powell. "Mrs. Powell, are you absolutely sure that the woman in there is your niece?"

"There's no doubt in my mind, Doctor," Gloria said. "She and Lindsay could pass for sisters if you didn't see them together, or ask their mothers. Lindsay is shorter. Nina is tall like the rest of the family. Lindsay has dark eyes and Nina had blue eyes. Nina's ears were prominent, but Lindsay had...has tiny ears. I wish I knew where she was." Her voice started to quaver, but she went on, "Other than that, their features were very similar." Tears started to slide down her cheeks. "I'm glad my sister isn't alive to see this," she repeated. The response in the room was silence.

Tunney's eyes sought Hollis's. "Mr. Haddon, Ms. Morgan, you two have been very quiet. Is there anything you'd like to add?"

Mark blew out his cheeks and shook his head. "Nothing that can't wait until morning; I need to digest all this."

Hollis nodded in agreement.

Dr. Fell committed to calling Tunney the moment he received the results. The group got up from their chairs and headed outside.

In the parking lot, Tunney faced them. "I expect you all in my office tomorrow at nine o'clock." He paused. "Make that eleven. I'm hoping that Dr. Fell will have the results by then, and we can talk with certainty."

Gloria protested, "But I know she's—"

"Please, Mrs. Powell, I don't doubt that you recognize your niece, but in cases like this where there's an incorrect death certificate, we have to move prudently and by the book." He glanced at the time. "Let's everybody go home and get some sleep. We'll get back together in the morning."

The ride to Gloria's home was silent. There were a few questions Hollis wanted to ask, but it was clear the older woman was not physically or emotionally ready to respond.

A short distance from their destination, Hollis cleared her throat. "Mrs. Powell, we can pick you up on our way downtown. But I wonder if it's possible to come a little early so we can speak with you. I'd like to ask you about Lindsay's whereabouts."

Mark shot Hollis a sharp look in the rearview mirror, but said nothing.

"I'm not sure I can help you, but yes, of course," Gloria replied. "I can fix breakfast—"

"No, absolutely not," Mark interrupted her. "We'll take you to breakfast."

Hollis remained in the car as Mark escorted Gloria upstairs. She moved to the front seat, and a few minutes later he bounded down the steps.

"Well, this has been a red-letter day," Mark muttered, driving onto the freeway. "What the hell is going on, Hollis?"

She shook her head. "I don't know. I feel we've been handed a bag of half truths, or least bad information, and asked to play a game where everyone else but us knows what's going on."

"So, Lindsay is alive."

She thought a moment. "Yes, and I think Gloria is talking to her now."

WHILE MARK PUMPED GAS, Hollis used the time to make phone calls. First, to Penny to check in and say she would be in the office in the morning.

"I'm wiped out," she said, "and for once I'm going to get home early. John is leaving day after tomorrow on an assignment."

"No problem," Penny responded, "though you may want to call Gordon before you call it a day. He didn't look happy. I'm supposed to tell you to see him as soon as you get in tomorrow."

"Thanks, Penny, I will."

Her next call was to John, to let him know of her change in plans. He was in a meeting and texted her back that he'd be packing for his trip and would be up when she got in.

Unable to think of anyone else to call, she punched in Gordon's number.

"Why didn't you bring me up to date before you left?" His irritation was evident.

"Hello, Gordon. I'm fine, thank you," she said calmly. "This was the first chance I had to call. We just dropped off Gloria Powell and Mark—"

"You're party to a dead body exchange involving your client, and you…and you find time to talk to everyone in the county but me." He muttered something under his breath. "I've been fielding calls from Florin. What the hell is going on, Hollis?"

She took the next few minutes to bring Gordon up to date. He let her speak without interrupting, or surprisingly, taking another call. When she finished, there was a brief silence.

"Okay, I see how this got off track. I'll handle Florin and the ME," he said. "Have your breakfast with Mercer's mother, Gloria Powell, and see me when you get back. I told Florin we would get her to coax Lindsay to make an appearance." He hesitated, and then said, "Although you didn't hear this from me, I'd be very careful. Someone out there is trying to kill your client."

TWENTY-TWO

ON THE DRIVE to the firm the next morning, Hollis went over in her mind the surprises of the previous day. There was only a little time before the meeting with Tunney. Gloria had called her late the night before, begging off their early-morning meeting.

"I'm sorry, Hollis," she said. "But I'm mentally and physically drained. Can we talk after our meeting with Mr. Tunney?"

Of course she agreed, and after informing Mark, was told he'd retrieve her from in front of the office building after he'd picked up Gloria.

Hollis thought over recent events. Lindsay's plan was to ensure that the money got to Gloria Powell without the threat of discovery. She had feared that the bad guys would notice her mother's increased fortune and either harass her or be able to track the money back to Lindsay and realize that she wasn't dead.

Well, Lindsay's plan led to the killing of her cousin. Perhaps it was time for another plan.

She looked up when DiFazio poked his head into her doorway.

"I was waiting for you to get in." He took a seat without waiting for her invitation. "Penny told me you went to the morgue to ID Lindsay Mercer. That must have been gruesome. How did it go?"

"She's dead."

He gave her a long look, and when she made it clear that she wasn't going to say anything more, he added, "It's going to be a lot on Nina Shaw's shoulders as her beneficiary." He shifted in his seat. "Well, I'm glad it's not my case. You know I'm willing to help you, even on the tough ones."

"Yeah, I know," Hollis replied.

They exchanged looks.

"You don't like me much, do you?"

Hollis hesitated before answering, "DiFazio, I don't know you well enough to like or not like you. You seem like an okay guy, but…but I'm not into sharing, and some would say that I don't play well with others." She held her hand up. "It's okay. I like working alone. I think that's why I like probate law. But until they're closed court cases, I keep my clients' affairs close to my vest."

DiFazio shrugged. "Well, then, I can report that I've gotten a handle on the last of all the cases you gave me to review, and I have an appointment later today with a new client hopeful. It's a standard trust." He paused. "Look, I'm not trying to steal your clients. I only asked about the Mercer Trust because it's intriguing."

"Really? Steal my clients?" She smiled and glanced at the time on her screen. "I've got an appointment at the DA's office this morning. Let's go over everything after your meeting with your new client."

He stood to leave.

"I guess I'm not saying this well, but Penny said you like working with Vince. If you ever need a professional, I can be of help, too."

"I'll remember that."

HOLLIS SAT ALONGSIDE Mark and Gloria in the district attorney's reception room, waiting for Tunney to make an appearance. She'd retrieved her notes from the office and left a confidential memo for Gordon. From the sign-out board, she'd learned he was going straight to court and wouldn't be returning until early afternoon.

While Mark and Gloria sat in silence, preoccupied with their own thoughts, she scribbled hers on paper, making a circular diagram of the unanswered questions.

Who killed Nina?

Were they really after Lindsay?

Where is Lindsay?

The list of possible answers and cross relationships under each resembled spaghetti.

"Looks like you all could use a cup of coffee," Tunney said, walking over to them.

Hollis quickly put away the page. "I drink tea. Are you buying?"

"We'll take coffee," Mark said.

"Good, follow me."

A conference room was equipped with a tray of water, coffee, tea—and a court reporter.

Hollis halted in the doorway. "If she stays, we're leaving."

"What's the problem?"

Hollis gave him a false smile. "I'm a newbie, but I'm not stupid. Unless one of us is a suspect in a criminal matter, we're not giving statements. We only came to be of assistance to your office, not to incriminate ourselves."

"I agree," Mark said from the hallway.

Gloria Powell, looking curiously from one to the other, moved to stand behind him.

Tunney pursed his lips and then nodded to the young

woman. "We won't need you this morning, Audra." As she left the room, he turned to his visitors. "Okay? Now, please come in."

They filed in and took seats, Tunney on one side of the table, Hollis, Gloria, and Mark on the other.

"First, let's get this out of the way," Tunney said brusquely. "I verified that Lindsay was in a witness protection program. She—"

"What made you think to check?" Hollis queried.

Tunney frowned. "What do you mean?"

Hollis stared at him. "I mean, do you assume that every dead body is in a witness protection program? Only a few people knew. It may be because Lindsay's participation was leaked that her cousin paid the price. I'm just curious: how did you discover that Lindsay Mercer was in the program?"

"Her name is on a watch list. The pertinent agency doesn't indicate the reason," Tunney responded with obvious annoyance. "Local law enforcement and the DA's office reference it when sensitive situations like this arise. Only top officials have access."

Hollis wasn't satisfied, but she didn't know what else to ask.

"Can we get started?" Tunney pushed.

"Just one other thing, Mr. Tunney," Hollis persisted. "What agency put her name on the list, and was there a contact shown?"

Tunney's face flushed and his jaw clenched. He took a breath. "The FBI was the agency, and I'll have to check with my contact there to see if I can disclose the name."

"Thank you." Hollis gave him her sweetest smile. "Now, we can get started."

Tunney turned back to the others. "Mrs. Powell, per-haps you could share your story. First, how long have you lived in California and how did you get to be here?"

Gloria cleared her throat. "Lindsay left Chicago three years ago, right after she gave her testimony. They put her on a plane, and I didn't know where she was for months. She would contact me through correspondence every month or so to tell me in code that she was okay, but not where she was. About six months ago, she told me that she was tired of living in fear of being discov-ered. She didn't trust the FBI anymore; she was going to plan her own disappearance. She would get in touch with Nina, because she needed her help to make sure I was taken care of. I was skeptical. Nina can't hold water; she's terrible at keeping secrets. She would never be able to keep Lindsay's situation confidential." Glo-ria stopped, seeming to realize that she should speak of Nina in the past tense. "Lindsay assured me that she wasn't going to tell Nina anything that could lead to her location."

"So, what was Nina doing here? Did Lindsay keep in contact with her?"

"I don't know. Lindsay never said anything to me."

"Did Nina tell you she was going to see Lindsay?" Hollis prodded.

"What? No, no, I told you, Nina didn't know where Lindsay was either," Gloria said. "But one time when Lindsay called me, I called her right back before she could get rid of the phone." She took a breath. "But like I told you, I traced her. I couldn't believe it. I had found my daughter."

Her eyes were brimming with tears.

"She said if things stayed quiet, she would come to

see me, and she did." Gloria smiled. "We reunited in Reno. She only stayed one night. I felt so much joy in my heart to see my baby again. We had a long talk. We wanted to be together, no matter what. To be safe, we waited three more months, and then I moved here." She looked down at her hands. "I made sure people thought that I was visiting friends in Florida, and I told my Florida friends I was in Indiana."

"Where's Lindsay now?" Tunney asked.

Gloria shook her head. "I don't know. I haven't seen her since Reno." She must have noticed Hollis's skeptical look. "No, it's true. I don't know where she is."

"But you've talked with her," Hollis said.

Gloria blushed. "Well, yes."

"When was the last time?" Tunney questioned.

"Uh, a short while ago. She told me she had a plan to disappear again. She thought her current identity had been leaked and she was selling the store. Then she said she was working with you." Gloria looked at Hollis. "That Ms. Morgan would contact Nina to make sure I had enough money. That…that it might be a while before we saw each other again, but that we would be together when she was settled."

"Wasn't she nervous about putting her cousin at risk?" Tunney asked.

"No. Nina left Ohio long before Lindsay got into trouble with the law." Gloria squared her shoulders. "She was estranged from her mother and the rest of the family. She wasn't real close to Lindsay either, so she made an excellent 'drop,' as Lindsay called her."

"And the fact that they looked alike?" Mark asked. He had been silent up to this point, but now he had both elbows on the table, hands clasped together.

Gloria's eyes shifted from side to side. "Until today, I never thought that...that she could be mistaken for Lindsay. She was supposed to stay in Ahwahnee." She turned to Hollis. "Not here. She was never supposed to be here."

Mark and Hollis exchanged looks.

"And what about you?" Tunney turned to Mark. "How do you fit into this whole thing?"

"I don't," he said. "I knew Lindsay for about three years: first as a client, then as a friend. I represented her in a business matter, then we discovered we both liked history and from time to time we would meet for lunch and share. I introduced Hollis to her a short while ago."

"Did you know Nina?" Hollis asked.

Mark shook his head. "I didn't even know *of* Nina."

Tunney lifted a single eyebrow. No one spoke. Then he looked up and leaned toward Gloria.

"Mrs. Powell, do you know where your daughter is?"

"No, Mr. Tunney, I don't." She added, "I wish I did. She contacts me; I don't have a way to contact her."

Hollis frowned. She's not telling the truth.

He put his papers in a stack and stood. "Well, now this case has shifted to the murder of Nina Shaw, not Lindsay Mercer. Mrs. Powell, I'm going to need you to sign a statement verifying your niece's identity." He gestured for them to leave. "It goes without saying that if any of you hear from Mercer, you should contact this office as soon as possible. She's still a critical witness. It's very possible somebody thought they had her on that slab."

Gloria gasped.

"Mr. Tunney, please," Hollis said, exasperated. She reached to squeeze the older woman's shoulders.

"Ma'am, I do apologize," Tunney said, clearly contrite. "That was thoughtless of me. Niece or daughter, I am truly sorry for your loss and the pain it must be causing you."

Mark shot him a disapproving look. "You have our contact information. Perhaps, if you come up with any new information, you will let us know."

Tunney nodded. "Yes, of course."

Hollis steered Gloria out the door and back to the car. The woman's face had lost its color, and she walked stiffly, apparently grateful for Hollis's assistance. The three of them were back in the car and Mark was pulling away when Hollis spoke up.

"Gloria, are you okay?"

"I…yes, I'm okay." She turned to look at Hollis in the backseat. "I… I'm… I guess I'm numb. My niece has been murdered and my only child is running for her life, and I don't know where she is."

"Is that true?" Hollis said.

"What do you mean? Of course, it's true." Gloria turned back to the front and looked straight ahead. "I have no idea where Lindsay is now."

"But she is supposed to call you, isn't she?" Hollis said. "You said earlier she contacted you on a regular basis. When she reads or hears the news that her cousin was found dead, she'll be contacting you."

"I don't know that," Gloria mumbled.

"When she does," Hollis placed her hand on the woman's shoulder, "tell her to get in touch with me. I can help her, and you. But I need to talk to her. Tell her, I think I know who the leak is. If I'm right, I can give her the leverage she needs to get her life back."

Gloria twisted in her seat again to face Hollis.

"Hollis, is that true?" Her voice brightened with hope. "Can you help her?"

Mark frowned in the mirror.

Hollis shrugged off her unease. "Yes, I think so. I need to talk to her and fill in a couple of blanks, but I'm pretty sure I can find out not only how to help Lindsay, but who murdered Nina."

TWENTY-THREE

Hollis, Vince, and Justin were sitting at a table overlooking the Oakland Marina. She had deliberately chosen a weekday to avoid crowds, and while she was slow to admit it even to herself, she could see if they'd been followed.

She ordered salad, and the two young men ordered everything else on the menu.

"Whoa," she laughed. "You two remind me of my brother. He never missed a meal and he never met a food he didn't like."

Vince gazed at her. "I didn't know you had a brother."

"Yup," she responded, making it clear that she was finished with the subject. She signaled for the server to come over. "I can only stay a short while; I need to get back to the firm."

She was close to her brother Joe, who was three years younger. He was back from military duty in the Middle East, a grade higher but more subdued and introspective. She was just glad to have him back.

"I always wanted a brother, but I have an older sister," Justin offered.

"I met DJ," Hollis said. "She seems nice. She cares for you quite a bit."

He shrugged. "I was a disappointment to my parents. I didn't get along well with the other kids in school, so it was kind of rough. Without any friends, I hung out by myself a lot."

"What about Phil Carson?" she asked.

Justin smiled. "Yeah, he's a good guy." Then he looked down at his hands. "But I don't see him so much anymore."

"So you turned to computers?" she said.

Justin nodded. "I love puzzles and I'm really good with figuring things out. You know, finding things."

Vince chuckled. "You mean hacking?"

"Yeah, but it didn't work the way I thought it would." Justin took a bite out of his sandwich. "When people found out I could break into computers, I had a lot of friends...for a minute. They thought that I didn't know what was going on, but I did. I didn't care. It was nice having friends, if only for a minute."

"Those weren't real friends," Hollis said.

"Hey, man." Vince patted him on the back. "I had plenty of friends, but the wrong kind. They introduced me to drugs, and my life was turning out to be a dark scene."

Justin perked up. "Did your parents give you a hard time? I kept telling mine to get off my back. It was bad enough trying to deal with...with being bullied."

Justin sounded so young. Hollis waited to hear how Vince would respond.

He looked out at the water, then said, "Naw, man, I never knew my dad, and my mom...my mom was sharing drugs with me."

There was silence.

"Hey, I didn't mean to bring everybody down." Vince grinned and slapped Justin on the back. "I'm okay now, and my mom's a lot better. She…she's going to be out soon."

"How…how did you make it through?" Justin's voice quavered.

Vince raised his eyes to look into Hollis's. "I found a real friend who cared," he said. "And my life started over."

Justin nodded slowly and faked a hit to Vince's arm with his balled fist. He gave him a pleading look.

"I could use a real friend."

WHILE HOLLIS WAS with Justin and Vince, Stephanie had left three 911 texts on her phone.

"It's me," Hollis said into the phone.

"Sorry, now *I* can't talk. I've just got a new assignment. Can you do dinner?" Stephanie asked. "You're not going to believe what I found out."

"Sure, where do you want to meet?"

"How about Maud's, right after work?"

With John out of town, Hollis was glad for the meet-up, but the three hours passed too slowly. The routine of going through DiFazio's work required concentration but was mind-numbing. She was distracted. She couldn't stop wondering about Stephanie's discovery.

BY THE TIME Hollis got home, she had only a few minutes to change clothes before her dinner with Stephanie. She frowned. Hollis didn't know what Stephanie had to tell her, but she was eager to run some other things past her friend. She slipped on a pair of jeans, a pastel-yellow T-shirt, and her favorite black linen jacket. She was almost out the door when her eye caught the blinking message light on the phone.

John.

"I miss you. Don't forget your promise. I'll see you in ten days. Love you."

Hollis smiled. His voice was like a bright lighthouse in a foggy sea.

When she got to the restaurant, Stephanie was already there.

"Being friends with you is never boring." Stephanie returned the hug. "I'm not real hungry so I'm ordering soup." She put aside the menu.

Hollis frowned. "You must have news if you're turning down a meal." She glanced at the menu. "I'll have soup, too."

The server took their orders and retreated.

Stephanie leaned across the table. "That's not Lindsay Mercer on that gurney in the morgue."

"I know."

"You know," Stephanie muttered, amazed. "How did you find out? I've been making myself crazy with how I was going to tell you, and you already knew." Her voice held a hint of disappointment.

"Don't be mad," Hollis said, patting her hand. "I only found out late this afternoon when her mother identified her niece instead of her daughter as the body in the morgue."

For the next ten minutes, Hollis talked Stephanie through the ins and outs of Nina Shaw's death.

Soup finished, Hollis dabbed her mouth with a napkin. "I need to talk to Gordon first thing in the morning," she said. "Not only am I facing attorney-client privilege violations, I don't know if Tunney is aware of the latest federal deal that Lindsay cut. This thing is getting way out of hand."

"Wow, I had no idea," Stephanie said, rubbing her chin. "So, it's Lindsay's *cousin* who was murdered. You've ruled out that she could have been the target. Obviously, you think that whoever did it thought they had Lindsay."

"That's the thought I had. Evidently there is a close resemblance between them. I'm sure that's what the sheriff's office is going to put out to the press." Hollis frowned. "How did you discover that the body wasn't Mercer?"

"You told me that she was in the witness protection program. When you told me about the questionable death certificate, it raised a flag. I didn't take anything for granted. I knew her prints had to be on file, and I know Dr. Fell's assistant. I got access to the deceased's prints. No match."

Hollis nodded, but she could tell that her friend was holding something back.

"There's more, isn't there? What else did you find out?"

Stephanie lowered her voice. "Have you ever googled Lindsay Mercer's name?"

Hollis squinted. "No, I never thought to."

"Well, I google everybody, especially someone I'm trying to track down."

"What did you find out?"

"Nothing, except I discovered that after I did, three tracers were put on my computer. One of the guys in the office is a computer nerd. He's got this thing about viruses and our office being hacked. He put a safety alert on my machine." She looked around. "I had him track the tracers. Two came from the feds: the FBI and

Homeland Security, but it was the third one that bothered me."

"What did your computer wizard say?"

"It's a deep plant, linked to a string of false servers,"
she said. "He got real nervous and said I needed to report it, but if I did, he would be in a lot of trouble. On
the other hand, if he scrubbed my machine, my new
friends would know, and we might miss the chance to
find out who did it."

Hollis put her chin in her hand. She was really
tempted to involve John, though that would put him
in a compromising situation. Mercer's plan of a phony
death certificate to cover the fact she wasn't dead had
fallen apart. Worse, soon everyone would know that
Nina, and not Lindsay, had been murdered.

Finally, her thoughts ran to the events that seemed to
be filling her notebook. Lindsay knew her mother was
here. Did she know about Nina's presence?

Stephanie sat quietly, letting her friend think things
through.

Hollis had a bad feeling in her stomach. "So what
did your tech guy end up doing?"

"He was hooked by the challenge. I told him not to
scrub my computer, but otherwise to go for it, and follow the server path to the end." She grimaced. "Whoever put that third tracer on my machine was on the
inside. It originated locally."

TWENTY-FOUR

HOLLIS WENT OVER her notes as soon as she came in the office the next morning. She couldn't get the implications of Stephanie's findings out of her head. It was clear that there was someone close by who was able to place digital markers on persons accessing Lindsay Mercer's information.

They knew Lindsay's witness protection program identity.

Hollis thought hard. She hadn't done any internet research on Lindsay—her work had all been original creation—but it wouldn't surprise her if Penny had done her usual thorough job of background searching.

Best not to alarm her.

Nor was she going to reveal that Nina Shaw, not Lindsay Mercer, was residing in the morgue.

While it was possible that Lindsay knew Nina was in the Bay Area, it was also possible that Nina had somehow been lured here. Did he, *or she*, know how closely the cousins resembled each other? Hollis didn't think so. Nina could have easily and quietly been murdered in Ahwahnee without anyone being the wiser. The killer was after Lindsay. They had to make sure she was silenced. Whatever cards Lindsay still held had to be neutralized. And then there was the money. They needed to have the trust processed.

Sadly, in all likelihood Nina would have been killed

anyway. Hollis had no doubt that the crooks, with their computer acumen, would somehow interject themselves into the flow of cash and divert it to their accounts.

At the moment, the killers thought that they had successfully killed Lindsay. But once Shaw's identity was known, Lindsay's fake death certificate might raise suspicions.

So, why had Nina come to the Bay Area? Hollis glanced at the time. It might be too early to call, but she had to stop the circular questions going on in her head. She needed answers.

Gloria Powell was already awake. She responded that she, too, had not been able to sleep and was sitting in her kitchen trying to make sense of it all. "No, no, Hollis. Your call came at a good time," she insisted. "Besides, I must tell you something."

Hollis sighed. "It seems we're both unsettled. What is it?"

"Lindsay called me close to midnight last night. She…she told me that she had worked things out with you and that I should expect to hear from Nina. I told her that Nina was dead and that I'd tried to locate her after we went to the morgue to tell her, but she didn't get back to me. Well, she was quiet a long time, and I knew she was crying. She said she'd killed Nina."

"What?"

"Oh, no, not directly," Gloria said hastily. "She said that Nina had contacted her. She wanted to meet face-to-face about being a go-between in her trust. Lindsay thought that it would be rude and presumptuous not to agree, since she needed her help."

Hollis let out a breath. "But by arranging to meet her here, Lindsay unwittingly set up Nina to be confused for her." This tragedy of errors was becoming clearer. "How did your call end?"

"She said she had to rethink her plans, and that she would get back to me."

"Gloria, when Lindsay calls you again, I want you to ask her to call me as soon as possible."

"All right, of course." She paused. "Hollis, do you know what's going on?"

She took a moment before replying, "I thought I did; now I'm not too sure. But I bet I know who does."

TWENTY-FIVE

"Ah, now I know what Eleanor is talking about." DiFazio entered Hollis's office and sat in front of her desk. "You do get in early."

"And yet, here you are, too," Hollis said. "What brings you in so early?"

"I wanted to finish up a few filings before...before I left for the day." DiFazio sounded wistful. Then his voice took on strength. "I'm a real good attorney, Hollis."

"I know," Hollis said. She pointed past him. "I didn't see your light on. How long have you been in the office?"

He sat down.

"Long enough to overhear your conversation with Gloria Powell," he said. "You thought you were alone, but you should have closed your door."

Had she known he was lurking in a darkened office, she would have.

DiFazio looked around and over his shoulder. "I used to have an office like this."

"In Chicago?"

He flinched. "Ah, you found me out. Once I got to know you, I figured it wouldn't take long." He rubbed his earlobe. "Well, if you know about Chicago, you know everything."

"No, not everything, but enough to know that you're going to go to prison for conspiracy to commit murder. You should have closed *your* door." Hollis leaned back in her chair. "Your résumé didn't ring quite true. And while Ed was impressed with your background, and you were only under contract, I couldn't help but wonder how someone as brilliant as you would be available for hire on a few days' notice."

DiFazio nodded in acknowledgment. "I told them it was too rushed."

"Did you commit her features to memory from that day you met her? It wasn't an accident, was it?"

He shrugged. "I'm not an evil man. They needed to know what she looked like since being in the program." He rubbed his hands on his pants legs. "Evidently she never bothered to change her looks. She still matched the photo they gave me."

"But you didn't realize that Nina Shaw was a look-alike?"

He shook his head. "What are the odds of that happening?"

"Lindsay wanted to say thank you in person to her cousin."

"So I heard." He closed his eyes briefly, and then opened them. "I was in the hole too deep. They had me by the neck, and they squeezed. They knew Mercer was living out here, but they didn't know where. Then one of the wives recognized her picture in a newspaper story about a fundraiser, and once they had the name she was using they were off and running. I... I had no choice."

"So they somehow got Ed to hire you here. But I haven't figured out how you knew that Lindsay was *our* client—that we were preparing a trust for her." It was the question that still had her guessing.

"We had her store's website, which led to accessing

her computer emails to a friend of yours, Mark Haddon. They put bugs on his computer, and eventually he referred her to Triple D. They worked fast. Using an attorney contact, they pulled strings, called in favors, and the rest you know." DiFazio shook his head. "I... I had my own reasons for disappearing. I'd built my own witness protection program. I left my job as a partner in a prestigious law firm, came out here, and worked in a small firm as an associate. But they kept an eye on me to use whenever they needed."

"And however they needed?"

"Yes, that, too." His face turned pale. "I... I was supposed to keep an eye out for Mercer and report her movements."

"That's why you 'helped' me prepare her trust," Hollis said with air quotes. "You had all the information you needed...*they* needed, and you found out about Gloria. But why did they kill Nina?"

"She wasn't supposed to be here."

Hollis flashed back to those same words that Gloria Powell uttered. Not taking her eyes off DiFazio, she slid her phone into her lap, hoping she was punching the right keys.

"Why are you so willing to say these things now? You're incriminating yourself," she said.

He gave a short laugh. "I want you to consider taking me on as your client."

"Ah, attorney-client privilege," Hollis responded. "Well, we both know that's not going to happen. So why?"

DiFazio leaned forward. "I'm not kidding, Hollis. I want you...well, not you *personally*, but maybe Gordon to take my case. Will you talk to him?"

She was amazed at his self-absorption. He was responsible for a young woman losing her life, and it seemed not to concern him at all.

"I'm not making any promises," she said. "Getting back to Shaw, Lindsay called her to come up and meet with her before she…she went away. Thanks to you, her tormentors knew the terms of the trust—they had addresses and contact information. So they mistook Nina for Lindsay and killed her. How were they going to get possession of the money?"

"You'll help me with Gordon?"

"You need to ask him yourself. Remember, we represent the woman you tried to kill; there's a major conflict."

"I'll waive it." As if to demonstrate, he waved his hand over the files on her desk.

She shook her head in doubt, but he continued to talk.

"Remember, they thought Nina was still alive. They were going to electronically intercept the transfer as soon as you released the account for distribution. The bank numbers were in the addendum to the trust."

Hollis could almost taste bile rising in her throat. "I know, I put them there." She would never repeat that procedure again. "So, Nina was marked."

"I tell you, I never knew they would kill her."

"I don't believe you," she snapped. "You had to know."

His voice rose, imploring. "I didn't know she had a cousin who was practically a twin. I confirmed the picture they gave me of Lindsay Mercer with the woman I saw that day in your office." He sighed, shoulders slumping. "Evidently, the shooter they sent mistook Shaw for Mercer."

"So they hired a killer? They went to a lot of trouble."

"It's a lot of money."

She thought a moment, and then frowned.

"Wait a minute…they brought you to Nina Shaw, didn't they?" Hollis's voice rose. "You identified on sight Nina as Lindsay, didn't you? Whether Shaw or Mercer, you were still willing to point her out."

"She…she was in the store," he sputtered. "I thought it was Mercer. They looked so much alike. I didn't know they would kill her. I didn't *know*. I thought they would just threaten her."

DiFazio's handsome features collapsed in misery. He repeatedly cleared his throat. She believed that he believed his story. It was probably the only way he could face himself.

Good liars are good actors.

DiFazio seemed to finally realize his situation. He stood up suddenly to leave but didn't make it to the door before Cook entered with two uniformed officers. DiFazio appeared to deflate. He was ready for them, and after acknowledging the Miranda warning, he held out his wrists for the handcuffs. He went without a word and only a nod in Hollis's direction.

He's been arrested before, Hollis thought.

"Don't forget to talk to Gordon," DiFazio said over his shoulder.

"I'll be talking with you later, Ms. Morgan," Cook said.

"I'll be here."

A small group of employees gathered in the lobby as DiFazio was steered to the elevators. Gordon was in court, but Ed Simmons caught her eye and signaled for her to follow him to his office.

She took the next minutes to brief him. Fortunately,

Gordon had kept him abreast of the Mercer case and the Shaw murder.

"I had no idea," he said, with a worried look on his face. "We needed someone in a hurry. I didn't question. He came with a recommendation letter from one of my oldest colleagues. I can't imagine that Gordon would ever consider taking his case."

Hollis knew Ed thought of himself as infallible, so she decided to remain silent. Cook would want to interview Ed's "oldest colleague" as well as all of them. There would be plenty of opportunities to discuss "if only." She left Ed still shaking his head to return to her own office.

Only one question remained. Where was Lindsay?

THE BUZZING WOKE her from a sound sleep. Its persistence was annoying until she realized it was her cellphone.

It was one thirty in the morning. She clicked it on. "John?"

"Hollis, it's me, Lindsay. I need to see you."

She blinked her eyes to clear her head. "I need to see you, too," she said. "When?"

"Now, if possible."

Hollis frowned. "Now?" She sat up in bed. "Where are you?"

"Meet me in an hour at the twenty-four-hour café across the street from the San Lucian main library," Lindsay said in a rush. "Do you know it?"

"Yes, I know it." She stifled a yawn. "I'll be there."

Lindsay clicked off.

Hollis pulled back the covers and proceeded to dress. Thank goodness John wasn't home. There would be no amount of rationalization she could use to convince him to let her meet up in the middle of the night with a woman who was under a death warrant. But then John wasn't here. She grabbed her car keys.

Belle's was a locals' café. Hollis knew it from the meetings of the Fallen Angels Book Club. It was tucked in the back of a strip mall. You had to know it was there because signage was minimal. The food was terrible and the service deplorable, but the coffee was strong. Its claim to fame was that it never closed, and for that reason, it always had a small, grudging crowd. It benefited from the employees of two nearby hospitals.

Lindsay was sitting in a booth in a small alcove. They didn't bother with greetings.

"I take it you've talked with your mother," Hollis said.

"Yes, she told me what happened. I was surprised about Leo DiFazio. They worked fast."

The server approached to take their order. Lindsay ordered coffee and Hollis hot water. She took out her own tea bag from her purse. Belle's tea bags had no labels.

"Your drama's over, isn't it?" Hollis asked.

Lindsay nodded. "I hope so. When did you figure things out?"

Hollis hesitated before speaking. "I think when your mother identified Nina's body. She mentioned that Nina had had a hard life. A small bell went off in my head, but so many things were not what they seemed that I couldn't put my finger on why that bothered me." She took a sip of her tea. "Nina worked for bad guys, didn't she?"

"Only toward the end. She thought she was craftier than they were." Lindsay shook her head. "My dear cousin, my dear *greedy* cousin, was ready and willing to give me up. She contacted me on a phone line I had told her never to use unless my mother was in danger or deathly sick. She wanted me to know that they had made her an offer if she gave me up, and would I be willing to match it," Lindsay said in disbelief. "Can you imagine?"

"Otherwise...."

"Otherwise she would lead them to me. She said she was coming to the Bay Area to meet me. I told her to stay away, that she was putting not only my life, but also my mother's at risk. She didn't care. She'd figured that she would get money one way or the other. She was tired of living 'hand to mouth'—her words."

"How ironic that she should die because of mistaken identity." Hollis gave a mirthless laugh.

Lindsay nodded. "To anyone who knows us, we don't really look alike. We resemble each other, like sisters, maybe, but to a stranger—"

"Like me?"

"Like you." Lindsay grimaced. "All they had to do was plant some fake IDs and the rest is history." Lindsay blinked away a tear. "My own cousin.... I trusted her. I couldn't tell Mom the true story."

Silence rose between them.

Hollis cleared her throat. "What are you going to do? There's no further need for the trust. Or, at least not the way it's written."

"No, when I found out about Nina's treachery, I realized that I was done running. I made contact with the Chicago bunch and negotiated a deal for the money and my silence. It wasn't a win-win—I had to give up a lot of the money—but it means peace of mind. I still don't trust them. I'm going on with my plans to relocate, only this time Mom is going to come with me." She looked down at her watch. "We leave in a few hours. That's why I had to see you now."

Hollis mustered a smile. "Well, have a happy life."

She lifted her cup to tap Lindsay's.

"Thank you, we're going to go far away," said Lindsay.

Hollis grinned. "Do me a favor and don't tell me where."

TWENTY-SIX

HOLLIS PEEKED OVER her menu at Stephanie, who seemed engrossed in the wine list. Her friend had lost weight and her usual buoyant personality was subdued. There was an air of melancholy about her.

They gave their order to the server and Stephanie forced a brief smile.

"So, the mystery of Lindsay Mercer is wrapped up." She raised her water glass in a mock toast. "What's going to happen to DiFazio?"

Hollis shrugged. "He's trying to cut a deal with the feds, but they might not need him."

"I know. Maybe he can go into the witness protection program," Stephanie said, chuckling.

Hollis laughed with her. "Very funny. I...."

Hollis was speechless. She was looking into the eyes of Dan Silva, who was heading straight for their table.

"What's the matter?" Stephanie frowned then turned to see what had caught Hollis's attention. Her eyes widened.

"Hello, Hollis," Silva said. "I was told you ladies were lunching here today." Dan pulled up a chair and sat down at their table.

He was dressed in a suit, so he must have come from work. He, too, had an air of sadness.

"Penny, no doubt," Hollis muttered.

"Yes, she's a very efficient lady," he said. He turned

to Stephanie. "I'm not stalking you, Stephanie, but we need to talk. You're not taking my calls."

"Dan, we've already talked," Stephanie said. "There's nothing more to say."

Hollis cleared her throat and said, "I think I should leave."

They ignored her.

Dan leaned over the table. "Well, I think you're wrong. I didn't realize how it must look to you when I asked for those…favors." He leaned toward her. "You were absolutely right. I was just thinking of my career, but—"

"Look, why don't I leave you two to talk this out?" Hollis was about to stand, but Stephanie covered her hand with hers.

"No, stay," Stephanie pleaded.

Hollis realized that her friend wanted her there so she wouldn't lose her resolve. She nodded and sank back in her seat, taking in every word as she pretended to marvel at the technology of a cloth napkin.

"It doesn't matter." Not looking at Hollis, he seemed to accept the arrangement and continued, "I'll get on the mic, if it gets your attention. I have a bad habit of talking inside my head. Unfortunately, it means that the person I'm talking to doesn't hear me. But hear me now: I wanted to push my career so that we could start talking about a future together. I didn't realize how it would look to you. All I wanted was to be able to offer you a future we would share in."

"Whoa," Hollis exclaimed, looking at the blank expression on Stephanie's face.

Slowly the meaning of Dan's words sank in, and Stephanie dabbed her eyes with the back of her hand.

"Dan, what are you saying?" she said.

His face looked grim. "Hollis heard me." He took Stephanie's hand. "I didn't think I'd need a witness. I wanted to talk to you in a romantic setting with just the two of us. But I'll take what I can get. I've been miserable these last days. It didn't take long for me to realize I'd be crazy to let you get away. I don't care if you never do another lab test. We can continue to take it slow until we're both on the same track, but I want us to start planning a future together."

Hollis shifted her stunned gaze from Dan's piteous face to Stephanie's. Her friend was beaming and color was returning to her cheeks.

"No more lab tests?" Stephanie gave a tentative smile.

"No more lab tests." He held up his hand. "I'll wow them on my own."

She reached for his hand. "Then count me in."

TWENTY-SEVEN

HOLLIS HAD JUST settled down at her desk when she heard a light tap on the door. "Enter!" she called out.

"Vince." Her eyes widened. "I didn't expect you to check in until tomorrow. Is everything okay?"

He wasn't wearing his new "professional" attire this morning. He was dressed in his usual faded jeans and a black Raiders T-shirt.

"Yeah," he said, slumping down onto a chair. "Everything is good. I'm going with Justin to Golden Gate Fields this afternoon. I had to come in and get an office cellphone. Penny went off the charts about me using my personal one for business."

"Horse racing," she murmured. "Be careful. Justin can be slippery, but you can't let him out of your sight unless he's back at home." Hollis tapped her lips with the tip of a pen. "Penny's right about the phone; we can afford to give you one."

Vince cleared his throat. "Uh… Hollis, I know we have to represent people because everyone deserves a defense. But…well, have you sat down and *really* talked with Justin? I mean we went out for a beer yesterday and didn't get back until late. He talks a lot and even more with beer."

"What are you getting at?"

"He was telling me all this stuff about how he was going to change his life and get out of the identity theft business. Justin thinks that stealing IDs is the only thing he's really good at. He saw some show that said this dude was arrested for computer hacking IDs, but when he got out of prison, he was hired by the company he stole from."

She shook her head. "Don't tell me he thinks that this could be some kind of career path."

Vince chuckled. "That's pretty funny. But, yeah, I think he does." His smile faded. "Not only that, he gives me the feeling that he doesn't have…doesn't have the best…." He struggled to find the right word.

"Integrity?"

"That's your word. I was going to say, honesty. He had me take him to a gelato place over in Jack London Square. He knew the owner, who clearly didn't want to be seen with him. But Justin was looking for some-body—he never said who. He just tried to play it off."

"Where in the square?" Hollis frowned.

Vince gave her the location.

"Where does the lack of honesty come in?"

"The owner dude was real nice to us, gave us each a free cone—probably to get us to go away. Still, as soon as he had his back turned, Justin reached over the coun-ter and took his Square device."

"You're kidding."

Square was an electronic reader that would allow a small business to accept customer credit cards by just plugging it into the store's iPhone, or iPad.

"And this was a *friend*." He shook his head. "Don't worry. I snatched it out of his hand and put it back."

She shook her head. "Besides the track, what have you got planned for today?"

"He wants to go back to the gelato place." Vince grimaced. "He's definitely trying to connect with some-body. Oh, and by the way, tell the cops that their tail sticks out like a red light. I can spot them and so can Justin."

"Good. Maybe they'll keep him alive."

"It's not likely the guys you're trying to catch will reach out if they know it could be a trap."

Hollis nodded. "Good point. This thing could go on forever. I'll mention it to Cook." Her lips thinned. "Be careful, Vince. Don't take any chances. Call me if anything happens. I'll be visiting the Eastlands to-morrow morning around nine o'clock. I'd like you to meet me there."

"Not a problem," he said. He glanced down at his phone screen. "I've got to go now. My new buddy is probably getting jittery."

FOR THE NEXT couple of hours, Hollis wrapped up sev-eral routine matters waiting for her attention. Penny popped her head in the door to say she was going out for a sandwich.

"Go," Hollis urged. "I'm on a roll. I should have a clean inbox by the time you get back."

She turned back to the dwindling stack of files wait-ing for her signature. A few minutes later, her phone buzzed.

"Yes, Ms. Kagan, how can I help you?"

"Ah…there was a shooting." Barbara Kagan swal-lowed. "Our officer was seconds behind him, but your client was…killed. He was taken to Seaton Hospital in Berkeley. I'll—"

Hollis clicked off, grabbed her purse, and ran out the door.

SEATON HOSPITAL WAS just off Ashby Avenue, on one of the more congested streets in the city. She had to leave a message for Gordon at the office when he didn't answer, and one on his cellphone as well. She was on autopilot. Hollis didn't remember how she drove to the hospital or maneuvered her way to the emergency parking lot, and by the time she entered the lobby, her brain was racing and she looked around frantically for the information counter. Instead, she spotted Kagan coming down the hallway, waving for her to follow.

"He's isolated in one of the emergency rooms," Kagan called out. She reached out and touched Hollis on the arm. "The police called Eastland's parents; they're on their way. You may want to wait for the doctor to finish with the medical report."

"Where's Vince?"

Kagan looked puzzled. "Who's Vince?"

"He's one of our employees," Hollis said, searching the faces of everyone in the corridor. "He was with Justin. He's got to be here."

Through double swinging doors, Kagan guided her to a large room half full of police and hospital personnel. Hollis's eye sought the gurney with the fully-covered figure and slowly approached.

"Hey, lady," a police officer called out.

"It's okay." Kagan waved him off. "She's his lawyer." She pointed to the covered body lying next to the wall and said, "This is Eastland."

Hollis's eyes went immediately to the long shape closest to her. She took a deep breath and moved tentatively toward the table. Her phone buzzed, but it wasn't Vince and she ignored it. The same officer who tried to intercept her came over.

He stood in front of Hollis, blocking her progress. Then he reached over and gently pulled back the sheet. "You know him?"

Hollis fought down nausea, and then her eyes opened wide and she took a step back. While the face and hair were sprayed with blood, she could still identify the gray T-shirt she'd seen him wear.

"Where's Vince Colton?" she murmured, as her heart resumed its regular beat. "They were together."

Another man came up to them. "I'm the officer in charge until Detective Cook gets here." He took out a notepad. "Who's this Colton? Could he have been the perpetrator?"

Hollis shook her head. "No, not at all. Vince Colton works for my law firm. He was assigned to stay close to Justin Eastland—to keep him out of trouble."

"Well, he did a bang-up job," the officer remarked, not looking up from his notepad.

"About as good as the professional police officer who was assigned to protect Justin," she snapped.

Her next retort was drowned out by the vibration from her phone. This time she glanced down and gasped. Vince.

His message was a simple: Need to C U.

Moving quickly toward the door, Hollis texted Vince to meet her in a café across the street from the hospital's side entrance. She arrived there first and sat anxiously looking out the window for his arrival. Her mind ran through a host of scenarios that lacked one thing—information.

Justin had been murdered.

EVEN AS VINCE APPROACHED, she could tell he was pretty shaken up. His shoulders were hunched over, and his face had a gray pallor. She waved at him, and he acknowledged her with a heavy nod.

"Vince, are you all right?"

She'd ordered a cup of coffee, which he grabbed like a life preserver.

"Yeah, I'm okay. I can't say as much for Justin, but I'm not hurt."

"Vince, Justin is dead."

"I know. He had to be."

Hollis waited a few minutes until he drank a little more, appeared to be breathing normally, and his hand stopped shaking.

"Can you talk about what happened?" she said softly. "We need to go see the police. They need a statement as soon as possible if they're going to catch whoever did this."

He didn't respond as he stared into his cup.

Her phone buzzed, and she picked up the call.

"Gordon, I'm with Vince."

She heard a sharp intake of breath. Gordon barked, "Where are you? Wait for me to get there before you let him talk to the police."

She gave him their location, and he said he wasn't far. He'd be there in minutes. She clicked off. The server had brought her more hot water for her tea and refilled Vince's coffee. Color was slowly returning to his face as he struggled to pull himself together.

"Gordon is on his way," she said. "You're going to have to repeat your story several times today, so we'll wait for him to hear it the first time." She peered at him. "Is there anything you want to tell me that you may not want others to know?"

He shook his head. "Nah, I can tell everything. What

there is to tell." He swallowed hard. "Do you think they'll try to pin it on me?"

"No," Hollis protested. "What would make you say that?"

"He's right to ask," Gordon said as he slid into the booth next to Hollis, tucking his briefcase under the seat, and at the same time motioning to the server to bring another coffee.

Hollis had never been so glad to see anyone. "Gordon, good you're here. Vince held off telling me his story until you arrived."

Gordon and Vince exchanged looks.

"Okay, young man," Gordon said, taking out a recorder and putting it in the center of the table. "Let's hear it from the very beginning."

Vince blinked several times then cleared his throat. "Justin started acting strange as soon as we left his house." He looked off into the distance. "He's a jumpy guy anyway, but this morning he was making *me* nervous."

"What time did you two leave his house?" Gordon asked.

"About eleven."

Vince ran his fingers through his hair. "He wanted to get to the track around one. But he said he had to go to his apartment first for his lucky jacket, and we wouldn't be more than five minutes. He told me to stay in the car, but I knew that if I let him out of my sight, Hollis would kill me, and I really didn't trust him. So I said I was coming up anyway."

He took a gulp of coffee. "He ran up the steps and opened the door. I was right behind him. But when I walked in, he was just standing in the middle of the floor with this blank stare, the blood…and…and I saw

a red stain on his chest spreading fast. And then he...
he just fell forward. I think I called out his name, but
then someone hit me on the back of my head. They must
have been standing behind the door. I was out cold...
I don't know for how long. It had to be almost a half-
hour. I woke up, and he was still there...on the floor."
Hollis could tell he was seeing the scene all over again
in his mind.

"He...he was still alive, but not much. I called 911
right then." Vince rocked slightly. "He lips were moving, and I bent down. I told him I'd called for help. He
opened his eyes to see me, and I think he tried to smile.
He repeated the word 'mug' or 'rug' or maybe 'thug,'
over and over. Then he closed his eyes and...nothing."

"Thug?" Gordon repeated.

Hollis frowned. "Maybe he was trying to say something about the killer."

"Maybe," Vince said doubtfully. He cleared his
throat and continued, "I knew he was dead. There was
a lot of blood, and I could tell. But I didn't touch him. I
didn't want to mess up evidence." He shook his head. "I
should have stopped him from going to his apartment.
The dude was waiting for him."

"Did you hear the shot?" Gordon asked.

Vince shook his head. "No, nothing."

"Like you said, maybe the guy was already there,
waiting." Hollis frowned. "Can you remember anything
about the man who shot him? I know you didn't see him,
but maybe his voice? Smell? Anything?"

Vince wrinkled his forehead in concentration. "No."

She had a quick thought. "Vince, are you sure there
was just one of them?"

He stopped and thought. "I... I think so. It's a small

place. Everything had been tossed. There's a bedroom, and someone could have been hiding in there, I guess. But I had the impression there was just the one guy."

"All right, at least you're safe now," Gordon said, turning off the recorder. "The outcome could have been much worse. Let's go check in. I don't want to be accused of withholding information in an active investigation."

CONSIDERING HOW DISMISSIVE she had been during their first encounter, Kagan took no time focusing on Hollis when they arrived at the hospital. Hollis introduced Vince, and Kagan told them to meet her back at the department.

At Cook's office, Hollis was surprised to find Tunney talking to the detective. Both looked up when Kagan motioned for her boss. She introduced Vince, and they all listened intently to Gordon as he summarized Vince's story. Tunney departed quickly, making it clear he wanted to be updated later. "We're going to need a written statement," Cook said, motioning to Vince. "And I'm going to call for an artist to sit with you and get your description of the room, how things looked. We've got photos from when we arrested him, but something could have been disturbed that would give us information now on what they were looking for. Anyway, it couldn't hurt. A lot of times the mind sees, but needs a nudge to remember."

Picking up his cellphone, he barked out orders.

Kagan edged Hollis to the side and whispered, "You should have told me you had an amateur babysitting Eastland."

Hollis was not in the mood to push back on the taunt

and ignored her. Kagan did not miss the snub, and her jaw tightened. Hollis eased back to Gordon's side.

Cook and Kagan took Vince to an interview room. Gordon and Hollis had chairs in the back. They sat quietly as the two pressed Vince for his memories of the man who had killed Justin. They asked the same questions different ways. Vince's face turned pale, but he didn't lose his nerve and shook his head.

"I never got the chance to see his face," he said. "Nothing stands out about him for me. It's kinda hard to—"

"Don't worry," Kagan broke in. "If he left any prints, we'll get them."

It wasn't until Vince had told his story for the third time that the group got ready to leave. It was late in the day. Cook stood and spoke at the door with an officer who had come to the room.

He returned to the table, closed his notebook, and tucked away his pen. "All right, Mr. Colton, we won't keep you any longer. We appreciate your cooperation and...."

Yet another uniformed officer entered the room and handed Cook a note. Hollis noticed a small frown come and go on Gordon's forehead.

"What's so important to interrupt your interview, Cook?" Gordon asked.

Cook ignored him and turned to face Vince. "Mr. Colton, it appears as if you are well-acquainted with our county facilities in Pleasanton."

Hollis stood. "Don't respond, Vince."

Gordon was already standing by her side. "This interview is over. Come on, Vince, let's go."

Cook waved them back. "Look, I had to bring it up,"

he said. "It goes to his credibility. However, I can tell you that we in no way think that Mr. Colton was involved in the murder of Justin Eastland. But he is our only witness, and he was the last person to see him alive. And before you write a letter to my boss, I know that his felony charges stem from juvenile court. Once you've been convicted, you're always going to be vulnerable to scrutiny."

Hollis gave Cook a sharp look, and turned to catch Vince giving her a reassuring nod.

One ex-felon to another.

HOLLIS SAT ON the sofa with her legs curled underneath her and a glass of Malbec in her hand. Her nerves were raw and her mind wouldn't turn off. John would be home in a little while, and she didn't want him to see her in her current state. As much as he resisted her protective handling of him, as he had already pointed out, he was a hypocrite and would do the same to her. She'd contacted him and briefly told him what had happened. He didn't like this situation, not one bit, and he wanted her to get police protection.

"I'm not on anyone's view screen," she told him. "It's Vince I'm worried about."

TWENTY-EIGHT

HOLLIS WOKE UP with a headache.

After the "talk" with John, she'd slept little. He was up most of the night, prepping for an important morning debriefing. It made no difference; she couldn't put to rest the events of the previous day. Coming into the office a little before dawn, she took scant solace in the clearing of the sky over the Berkeley hills as the sun started its ascent.

"I thought you might get in early," Gordon said, walking into her office an hour later. "Ed wrapped up the DiFazio matter. Moving on, there's a fair amount of paperwork to process. I'll have my paralegal take care of that. But I need you to meet with Vince and get him to give you a background accounting on his activities and conversations with Justin. You think about it, too."

"Just in case Justin told him something?"

Gordon nodded. "I don't want to do the DA's work for him, but the Eastlands are mentally wrecked. I met with them late last night. Their only son is thought to be a murderer, and then *he's* brutally murdered. The cops are going to label this matter closed." He tossed a file on Hollis's desk. "There may be nothing we can do to clear this case. But I don't want to sit on a chance to try."

Hollis focused on the preliminary police report. She set her jaw and began to read.

"I THOUGHT I told you to stay home today," Hollis chided.

Vince was slouched in a chair, bleary-eyed and dressed for work.

"I needed to come to work. Otherwise I'd make myself crazy."

Hollis understood the feeling. Work was her mental stabilizer and go-to battery charge.

"Well then, are you up for talking about your contacts with Justin?" She came from around her desk and sat in the chair next to him. "Gordon wants to give the Eastlands closure about their son before this matter gets put to bed. They need us to give them peace of mind—if that's possible."

He shook his head. "Uh, I don't know anything more than I already told you. I didn't really get to know him that well."

"Go back to when you two were going out for a beer. You said that the more he drank, the more he talked. What did he talk about?"

Vince wrinkled his brow in thought. "Before we even got there, on our way to the bar—we went to the sports bar over on Hesperian Boulevard—he went on and on about how the kids in high school would bully him because he was kind of nerdy. Then he told me that's when he got heavy into video games and computer hacking." Vince shifted in his seat. "He didn't call it that, but he made friends by changing their grades and giving them advance copies of the exams. And, hey, he wasn't bullied anymore."

"Where did he go to high school?"

"San Lorenzo High. We passed by it on our way to the bar—that's what made him think about it. Anyway, he went on to talk about how hard it was for him to get a job he liked, because he didn't have any real skills except hacking. So he connected with some old buddies from high school, who turned him on to the crowd that got him into trouble."

"Did he give you any names?"

Vince grimaced. "Yeah, he mentioned a couple of dudes with the street names of Beau and Cannon. But I couldn't say if they were the ones from high school or later, and I didn't want to ask for their real names."

"Okay, go on." Hollis wrote down the names.

He continued, "Anyway, he said he realized that he wouldn't make any real money unless he stepped up his game. By this time, he'd had two back-to-back beers and was talking nonstop. Half of it was bragging about the computer raids he did, the other half was about the money to be made in stealing IDs. But after the third beer, he started to get paranoid. He was looking around, as if someone could hear him."

"Was anyone paying attention?"

"Hell, no. The bar was over half empty, and no one was even close to where we were sitting. Even so, he lowered his voice so I could barely hear him, and he said that he had insurance."

"I take it he didn't say what kind?"

Vince shook his head. "Nah, but I got the feeling it was some kinda *thing*, you know. I mean it wasn't… it wasn't information, but maybe some kinda proof."

Hollis was silent. Justin was an unreliable source for information, and there was a good chance that his veracity didn't improve with alcohol in his system. She thought back to a conversation they'd had when she got the feeling that he was holding onto information or goods from the Nike bag that might give him leverage.

"Could it have been a data stick?"

"I don't know. Maybe."

"Is that it?"

Vince took a deep breath. "Yeah, pretty much. After that, he just kept repeating the same stories. I didn't want to sit there and encourage him to get drunk, so I told him I'd see him today and took him home."

"Was police surveillance there when you left the bar?"

He nodded. "What do you want me to do now?"

She gave him a worried look. "Be careful."

VINCE SAID HE would be just fine working in the mail-room for the rest of the day.

"It's not like it requires any complicated thinking," he said, more than a little offended.

Hollis shook her finger at him in feigned reproach and went down the hall to update Gordon, but he was on the phone and signaled for her to come back. Returning to her desk, she called to set up an appointment with Cook. He needed to hear about Vince's last talk with Justin. She felt a gnawing concern in her chest. If the man Justin was running from—the one who killed him or had him killed—thought that Justin told Vince something that could incriminate them, Vince could be in real danger.

Hence her new worry.

But she knew him. Once he got over the shock of being at a murder scene, he'd want to stay involved. He'd think it was training for his career in private detecting.

Penny knocked on her open door.

"Everybody heard what happened to Vince yesterday. It's all over the news, and some reporter has already been here trying to find him." She stood in front of Hol-

lis's desk with folders in hand. "Ed chased him away."
Penny waved her hand. "I wasn't worried; I knew he'd
never locate the mailroom."

Hollis fought down her questions. Even though Ed
Simmons was the head of the law firm and oversaw
most aspects of public relations, he hated the press in
all of its forms. The confrontation with the reporter
probably made his day.

"Did you go to the crime scene?" Penny frowned.
"Was it pretty bad?"

She shook her head. "I didn't see it, but I heard it
was bad."

"Is Vince in danger? The news said that they had a
witness. Were they talking about him?"

The press.

Hollis couldn't help but groan. "Can you get me a
Chronicle?"

"Sure." Penny turned and hurried away.

Hollis left her office and walked quickly to Gordon's
doorway. He was off the phone and reading the paper.
She knocked, walked in, and sat down.

"There's nothing like having a target on your back,"
Gordon said without looking up from the news page.
"Where is he?"

"Working in the mailroom."

"Let's get him up here. We need to talk." Gordon
pushed the intercom and gave directions to his secretary. He looked at Hollis. "He was working for us when
he put his life on the line." He slapped his desk with
the newspaper. "Damn, it was my own ego that had to
have an edge for another court win. That young man
didn't need this."

Hollis nodded in agreement. "I was carried away,

too. I wanted to win my first criminal case. I wasn't really thinking about Vince."

"Well, it ends now. Florin thinks they have a good chance to make a case. It's not bulletproof, but that's their job, not ours," Gordon said. "We're getting out of the undercover business. I'll arrange for Vince to give a video statement—"

"Won't the defense object to not having the chance to cross-examine?"

"That's the DA's problem. If they want Vince to give evidence, they've got to assure him that he won't have to tie up his life waiting for court dates. The video, that's it, that's all they're going to get. I'll—"

He stopped speaking and stared at the distraught woman standing in his doorway, wringing her hands.

"Marjorie, what's the matter?"

"I went to the mailroom because Vince didn't answer the phone," she said, looking like it was all she could do to hold herself together. "It gets loud down there, and I thought he might not have heard. So…so I went down." She was breathing hard and almost couldn't continue. "The…the mailroom was completely ransacked, mail crates and envelopes everywhere. And there was blood."

Hollis stood and went up to the woman, putting her hand on her arm. "Where was Vince?" she said in rising alarm. "What happened to him?"

Tears poured down the secretary's face and she sobbed, "Vince… Vince is gone."

TWENTY-NINE

"EVIDENTLY, THEY TOOK him out through the lower garage," Cook stated matter-of-factly.

Hollis and Gordon joined him in the firm's conference room. It took less than an hour for the cadre of uniformed police officers to question Triple D's staff and the building's other occupants who had access to the mailroom.

Hollis's jaw was tight, her outrage simmering just below the surface.

Cook continued, "A security guard saw him walking through the garage with another man and didn't think anything of it. Vince and the man appeared to be headed to the man's car. Of course now, thinking back, he said that Vince didn't return his greeting, which was unusual for him."

She cleared her throat. "What are his chances?"

Cook shrugged. "They didn't kill him outright. He's been kept alive. So he must have something they want, or they think he has something."

"Could it have been the same guy who said he was a reporter?" Gordon asked.

"We think so, so that's actually a bit of good news. The guy was wearing a disguise. When Simmons spoke with him, he described a man with a short beard and thick glasses. That matches the description the guard gave us. We found some makeup putty remnants on the elevator panel. Vince must have struggled and touched the guy's face or something." He paused. "Anyway, that means Vince might be allowed to stay alive until they get what they want." He looked away. "But they won't want him to be able to identify his captor if he's set free."

"*When* he's set free," Hollis insisted. "What happens now?"

"Look, like I told you before, we're pretty sure it's a criminal element run by a thug named Hammond. He's been around a while, but is new to California. He's mostly got his fingers into property crimes, and so far, he's avoided killing anybody."

Gordon shook his head. "He may be turning a corner. He had Justin Eastland killed."

Hollis winced.

"We work the evidence," Cook went on. "My team is already tracking them. They can't afford to keep Vince Colton too long. He either knows something or he doesn't. They'll let him go. These guys don't want this to go any further than it has to. They're feeling our heat close behind, and Hammond can't afford to lose face among his peers. They'll want to go back under their rock where they were before. But maybe this time we can catch them."

Gordon nodded. "What about the blood?"

Cook grimaced. "Well, there was a fair amount, and we don't know who it belonged to. There were drops in the elevator and the garage. We'll run some DNA tests, but that's going to take time. Still, since they both walked out under their own power, the wound must not have been too serious."

Hollis tried to shake off a sinking feeling. She was responsible for bringing Vince into this mess and now his life was in danger. He had no way of telling them where he was. He could already be dead. She closed her eyes for a moment, then they flashed open.

The phones.

"Detective Cook, don't cellphones have some kind of tracking thing?" Hollis rushed. "Couldn't you locate Vince by tracing his phone?"

Gordon looked at Hollis with new respect. "She's right, find the phone and find him."

"That's common knowledge." Cook shrugged. "Nowadays, the first thing an abductor does is take the phone. They know about the SIM card, too."

"Vince is a survivor," she insisted. "He had *two* phones, one from our office and his personal phone. I know him. He would only have given up one phone."

"Give me those numbers," Cook ordered. "I'll get an officer on it right away."

Hollis quickly scribbled them down.

"Good thinking." Taking the slip of paper, he said, "Let's hope he still has one of these phones on him." Cook punched a number into his phone and gave instructions to contact him with regular updates. He added, "I'm headed back to the department. Remember, if they get a hit, contact me immediately." He turned to his listeners. "I've got to go. I'll let you know if we make a connection."

"*When* you make the connection," Hollis pushed back.

HOLLIS WAS GLAD to have some time at home alone. John said he was running late, and until Vince was back, she couldn't focus. As she sat in Gordon's office, an idea had come to her. Was there anything Justin had told her that could lead to what the bad guys wanted?

She stared out the window.

Why hadn't Cook called?

She picked up her phone and glanced at the screen. *Nothing.*

She heard a key in the lock.

"Hey," John said as he bent down behind her and planted a soft kiss on her upturned lips, "what's with all the paperwork?"

"It's Vince's statement and my notes from conversations with Justin. I brought it home to give me something to do."

He sat next to her, and she quickly updated him with the outcomes from the day and the hope for the cell-phone GPS. John listened intently, and when she finished, he seemed lost in thought. Hollis nudged him.

"Do you think he has a chance?"

John looked into her eyes. "Yes, yes, I do," he said. "But I'm worried about something else. When he doesn't give them what they want to know, there's a good chance they'll be coming after you. Like I told you earlier, I think you should ask for police protection."

She sighed, and then nodded unhurriedly. "I'll keep that in mind. But I don't know any more than Vince. If I did, I would have given Hammond up long ago. I've got to figure out where Justin would have hidden that data stick."

He put his arm around her and drew her close.

"I don't suppose it would do any good to tell you to leave things to the police?"

Hollis snuggled closer. "For anyone but Vince, I would pull back. But he's my friend, and I'm the one who got him involved in all this. I... I can't."

John sighed in understanding. "Then it's going to be a long weekend."

THIRTY

VINCE WOKE UP and shivered. It was cold.

They had shoved the ski mask on backwards over his head, and it itched painfully. The bristles of wool brushed into the cuts on his cheeks and lips, and he could smell and taste the metallic tang of his own blood. It was hard, but he could still breathe.

And he knew where he was.

They had brought him to an abandoned building along the estuary in Oakland. Even in the almost complete darkness, he recognized the sound of water lapping against the rocky, so-called beach. He would never forget the moldy smell of these boarded-up rooms.

He'd slept here when he got high.

He chuckled.

He was high now.

They must have given him what they thought would be an overdose, but he was a former junkie, so it would take a lot more to kill him. The marks on his arms had pretty much faded, and in their hurry, they hadn't noticed.

He grinned. That meant that being a junkie was a good thing. It had saved his life. Wait until he told Hollis.

He frowned, *Hollis*.

She would be royally pissed off. He hadn't called her. His phone.

Would she remember?

The phone. It was in his leg pocket.

He'd turned it off, but the battery would be almost dead. It was a chcap one.

Cheep, cheep, cheep. He could hear the gulls flying overhead.

He tried to move his legs, and he screamed out from the pain. It cleared his head. Then he remembered. They'd broken one.

Another good reason for being a junkie. It covered up pain.

Not all pain.

Katie.

There was something he was supposed to remember, something about the kid.

Something....

He'd used the pain from moving his leg to trigger the memory.

Something....

Cheep, cheep, cheep.

He giggled.

He'd close his eyes for a minute, then he'd try to remember.

THIRTY-ONE

HOLLIS CAME INTO the office on Sunday. For once, John had encouraged her.

"You're no good here. I agree, go to the office. You're not going to rest, and at least you'll be in your natural environment," he said, a worried look on his face. "Vince is street-smart. He knows how to take of himself."

Tell that to a shooter.

The day before, she had called Kagan, then reluctantly Cook, but neither had any news of Vince, and both made it clear that they would call her if they did.

The waiting was almost intolerable.

The only thing higher than her frustration level was probably her blood pressure. She pulled out her notebook and started from page one and her first meeting with Justin. After poring over every line, she concluded that if there was something there, she couldn't find it.

Hollis opened her briefcase and took out a small envelope she'd retrieved from Justin's parents; it held the keys to his apartment and car. She punched in a text and didn't have to wait long for a call back. She quickly made her request.

"Ms. Morgan," Cook said tiredly, "what are you doing? It's Sunday, my only day of rest. Why do you want entry to Eastland's apartment? It's only under tape until tomorrow. Wait until then."

"Please, Detective, if you are going to release his apartment tomorrow anyway, what harm can I do? I just want to see for myself, that's all. Until Vince is back, I need to stay involved. I can't just sit around. If I discover anything, I will call you first."

There was silence.

"All right, all right," he said. "You've been helpful to us. But no cowboy stuff. You contact me right away if anything catches your attention."

"Thank you."

She picked up her purse and coat.

JUSTIN LIVED IN a low-income, mixed-urban neighborhood in San Lucian, just on the city limit line with San Lorenzo. A large group of kids were playing dodge ball in the street. There was a single-family house with a car parked on the lawn, and nearby yards reflected various degrees of care. His building was a fourplex located on the corner across from a small auto-repair shop home conversion, which may or may not have been permitted under city codes.

Slipping under the police tape, then using her keys, Hollis entered the upstairs unit and closed the door behind her.

It was a surprisingly airy one-bedroom unit, despite the disarray caused by the killer and the police forensic investigations team. It had little furniture and even fewer personal items. She opened cabinets and closets, not knowing what she was looking for. There were only three mugs and they were empty. His computers were gone. Cords lay in a pile on top of the kitchen table. The emptied drawers of the end tables next to his bed were pulled out and lay on the floor.

She stood in the center of the room and looked around for several minutes. Then she smiled. She had spotted a small, fringed area rug, rolled into the shape of a sausage and propped against the wall next to the linen closet. Kneeling on the floor, she flattened it out. It was a six-foot-long, high nap, round rug with coarse net backing. Slowly and carefully, she felt around the edges. She was almost halfway around when she felt what she had wanted to find—a small pocket.

Rug, not thug.

A space meant to hold a very small device. Justin had created a pocket by slicing into the thickness of the rug between the loops of fringe. He'd tried to tell Vince with his last whispered gasp at the end of his life to look at the rug.

Except the makeshift pocket was empty.

Hollis sagged. She'd been on the right track, except that someone had gotten there first. Who? Certainly not the police, so it had to be Hammond. Justin had held on to the last piece of leverage he had—if he was to be believed, a data stick. She had an idea what was on it, and she was sure her client had tried to play both sides to see who would give him the best deal, the good guys or the bad guys, or the other bad guys. Scrambling to her feet, she thought about what to do next as she rolled up the carpet and replaced it in the corner. She reached for her phone.

"Gordon," she said breathlessly. "I think I know what Justin's leverage was. What he took out of the Nike bag."

"Where are you?"

She took a breath. "I'm at his apartment. Don't worry, Cook knows. Justin said he still had leverage.

In his world, it had to be a computer file of some sort. I found his hiding place, except for one thing."

"What?"

"It's gone. But I—"

"Hollis, get out of there," he urged. "Go home. I've got to pick up my family from church, and I'm already running late. I'll see you in the office tomorrow." He paused. "I know you're worried about Vince. However, you'll do him no good making yourself crazy and definitely not if you're discovered by the wrong people."

She was only half listening because there were footsteps coming up the stairs.

"Gordon, I think I hear someone. I'll call you back."

She clicked off and put the phone in her purse.

The knob began to slowly turn.

She ducked behind the kitchen counter and sat on the floor with her back to the cabinets, but she could see through the open side shelves. It was a dark-haired young man, looking to be in his twenties, dressed in jeans and a T-shirt. Entering the apartment, he closed the door behind him. He was talking into a phone.

"I'm in," he said, holding the cell to his ear. "What am I looking for?"

Hollis held her breath, knowing it would be seconds before she was discovered. She moved her phone to her pocket. Taking a deep breath, she coughed and stood, clutching her purse to her chest.

"Holy shit," the youth cried out, backing up to the door. "There's someone else here. I don't know…some chick." He was of average height with brown eyes and thick, bushy brows. His nose and lips had a purplish hue as if he was a heavy drinker, and the lines in his face said he was burning the candle at both ends.

He pointed at her. "You aren't going anywhere."

"That's where you're wrong. Here's my purse. Take what you want."

She threw it at him and made a dash for the door. He grabbed at her purse, but it fell to the floor, its contents spewing.

"Wait," he growled, reaching out to grab her arm. He spoke into the phone. "What should I do?"

She squirmed violently, but couldn't pull loose from his grip. She could hear the sound but not the words of the voice on the other end.

"Just let me go," she cried. "I'm Justin's girlfriend. He sent me to get some of his clothes."

"You hear that?" the young man yelled. "Tell me what you want me to do."

"Help!" she screamed toward the door. "Help me."

"Shut up!" he barked, clearly uncertain what to do next.

"Help!" she shouted.

He threw her to the floor and backhanded her across the face. She cried out and rolled out of his reach. The pain surprised and silenced her.

"Yeah, I got it," he said into the phone. He clicked off and tucked it in his pocket.

He looked down at her, and she saw his sick grin.

"Got to take your picture," he said. "Nothing like having a hostage to say that we mean business."

He held up his phone.

"Are you nuts?" she said, rubbing her jaw. "Is that what your friend on the phone told you to do? Because I can tell you, he's selling you out." She scooted on her bottom to a corner. "You'll be holding proof of a federal crime, and when they catch you—because they will catch you—you'll be locked up for the rest of your life."

"I said to shut up."

He took her picture, but he looked concerned. Hollis pulled herself up.

She cleared her throat. "Look, I don't know who you are, and I don't care. I just came to get some clothes for my boyfriend." She spoke low and slow. He didn't appear to handle pressure well. "Does he owe you money? He owes me, too. I won't—"

Just then his phone buzzed. He looked at the screen, then at her.

"You almost had me fooled," he sneered. "I sent my friend your picture. He says you're workin' with the cops."

Hollis frowned. "Your friend knows me."

He put his phone away.

"I guess so. So now things are going to go a bit different." He reached behind his back and pulled out a pistol. He motioned for her to move toward the door.

"I'm not going anywhere with you. You're going to kill me anyway."

"He said you'd say somethin' like that."

He approached her with one arm upraised and the other holding out his hand.

"Gimme your phone."

Hollis hesitated, and her eyes flicked toward the door, judging the distance. He must have noticed her glance, because he shifted his stance to block her line of sight. She reluctantly slipped her hand into her pocket and handed him her phone.

"What happens next?"

Putting it in his pocket, he made a poor attempt at

a smile. "First, you're going to get on the floor and put everything back in your purse—now."

She got on her knees and reached for her lipstick.

"Wait, show me each piece before you put it in."

As she slowly held up each item, he nodded, then she carefully lowered it into the bag.

"Hurry up!" he yelled. "We don't have all day."

Saying nothing, she finished and held out the purse to him.

"Put it on the floor, over there." He motioned to a spot about four feet away—and out of her reach. Frowning, he held his phone and punched in a number with the same hand. He didn't take the gun off her.

He spoke into the cell. "Okay, I made her go through her purse, but she doesn't have the data stick." He nodded as if the person on the other end could see him. "Got it." He clicked off, motioning with his head to Hollis. "Take off your jacket, throw it on the counter, and empty all your pockets."

"I can tell you right now," Hollis said as she pulled out her pockets, "I don't know anything about a data stick." He frowned. "If you don't have it, you know where it is."

"No, actually, I don't."

Hollis's face still throbbed from his hit so she proceeded in silence. His growing frustration was evident as he shifted from one foot to the other and started to shake with agitation. Other than a pen and tissue, her pockets were empty.

He put the phone back to his ear. "It ain't here. What do you want me to do with her?"

Hollis could hear the sound of a response on the other end.

"What about the data stick? I came here earlier, and it's not in the rug."

At his words, Hollis's heart raced.

Her captor never took his eyes off her while he listened, then a slow smile crept across his face. "Not a problem," he said and clicked off, returning the phone to his pocket.

Hollis steeled herself for what she knew would certainly be unpleasant.

"Let's get goin'," he said. "You're comin' with me."

"Why? I don't know anything. I'm not working with the police. Justin Eastland was my client. I'm his lawyer. I'm just here to pick up his things for his parents."

He snorted. "Well, he's dead. He ain't goin' to need any clothes." He raised his hand. "Now I'm tired of talkin', and we have to go. Do I have to hit you again?"

"I promise," she responded, hoping she sounded on the verge of tears. "I'll come along without any problem. Just don't hit me again. But I'm confused. Could you tell me what it is you're looking for?"

"Don't talk!" he yelled, wiping his forehead with his sleeve. "You're going to come with me anyway, or I'll have to hurt you. Let's go. The truck is outside in the back."

Hollis looked down at her feet and nodded. "All right, I'm going. Please don't hurt me."

She walked in front of him but only enough so it would look like he was still by her side, instead of prodding her forward with the gun at her back. She gauged the distance to the street as they walked down the exterior stairs to a narrow corridor in the shadows. She might have a chance to escape when they reached the landing.

Her heart beat rapidly, and just as her foot touched

the last step, she turned, shoved him backwards, and took off toward the street. Cursing, he grabbed at the heel of her shoe—just enough to throw her off balance so that she fell onto the concrete. The palms of her hands and her wrists took the force of the fall as she braced herself. The pain was sharp and she fell to her knees.

"Help!" she screamed.

He was on her in seconds, covering her mouth with his hand. She bit down on his fingers, but he didn't release her.

"Bitch, I told you I would hurt you if you didn't act right," he snarled into her ear. "Now, you're goin' to make me hurt you bad."

He pointed the gun at her crotch. Her eyes grew wide, and she loosened her jaw. But he didn't take away his grip.

"Now, I see I got your attention."

Pulling her up to stand next to him, he shoved her toward the rear of the building and the parking lot.

He growled into her ear, "You make one sound or try to run, and I swear I'll shoot you in the back."

She kept silent.

Her mind raced, searching for possible escapes from his prodding gun. She could hear yelling from the house behind the fence next to the lot, but other than that, there was no one in sight. His pace quickened as a white delivery van parked near the entrance came into view. It was just a few steps from the building, and he deftly held Hollis's wrists together while he opened the rear doors. He pushed her inside, keeping his grip, and then followed behind.

As she struggled to right herself, he reacted swiftly, slamming the gun against the back of her head.

Then there was only blackness.

THIRTY-TWO

HOLLIS LIFTED HER head and felt an overwhelming sense of dread. How long had she been here, wherever "here" was?

It was dark and wet, and silent. When she tried to sit up, her head felt as if it contained a thunderstorm. The pain made her nauseous. Still, she managed to get to her feet. She stood in place until her head stopped swimming and the dizziness passed.

Her hand went to the large, throbbing lump behind her ear and came away with blood. He must have driven her in the van to this place and dumped her. She was alone. How long before John missed her? Gordon would notice she hadn't called him back. He'd contact Cook. They'd start to search for her.

She wondered for a fleeting moment if this was what they'd done to Vince.

She repeatedly blinked her eyes, trying to clear her head. There was no light except for a sliver that appeared to be coming from under a door.

A door.

With her arms outstretched, she cautiously took small steps toward the light. Her feet sloshed in her flats as she made her way through puddles of water. Finally she felt the frame of the door and her fingers sought the handle.

There was only a cover plate.

Her heart sank. She was the hostage, or prisoner, or worse of Justin's killer. To steady her nerves, she bit her bottom lip and gritted her teeth. Well, she was still alive, and they had kept her alive for a reason.

They thought she had the data stick, or could get it.

In the dim light, she gingerly walked and felt along the walls, trying to get a sense of the size of the room. It wasn't large, maybe the size of a storeroom or a medium-sized office. The walls were peeling plaster and as damp as the floor.

She stopped. A flock of gulls passed over. She must be near the Bay. They had kept her in the Bay Area, somewhere along a shoreline. Was it day or night? A thought came to her, and she reached inside her jacket before she remembered giving the man her phone.

Minutes passed, maybe an hour.

She heard approaching footsteps that echoed in the emptiness.

Her heart sank even further.

The door slammed open against the wall, and she jumped. Light assaulted her eyes, and she held her hands up to cover them. Whoever stood there said nothing. He grabbed her arm and pushed her out the door. It was a man.

Except for a small moan that escaped her lips when her head was jarred, she said nothing.

She didn't resist. She was finally out of that godforsaken room. Slowly, as he half dragged her steadily onward, she could tell they were in a warehouse. Windows were placed toward the top of high ceilings, and large bay delivery doors lined one side of a rectangular-shaped building. The other side had lengthy tables or maybe conveyor belts.

248 THE IDENTITY THIEF

Her captor wore a ski mask, and more importantly carried a gun, which he shoved into her left side.

He must have gotten some sort of indication or maybe heard or didn't hear something that should have been there. At any rate, he began to hurry and to pull her behind him.

"Where are you taking me?"

He answered with a push, and she staggered.

Finally they came to an open but much smaller area that had several closed doors leading out. Hollis's head was gradually clearing. She squinted, trying to focus on the back of her captor's head, some detail she would recognize later when she would have to provide a description. The thought actually cheered her by strengthening her resolve: she had no intention of dying here. Her eyes went to his shoes—they had red soles. She supposed they were the Louboutin version of athletic shoes. Her mind swirled. She'd seen those shoes before.

She remembered.

He pulled her arm toward the last door on the end. It had a large throw bolt, and he quickly slid it back to reveal total blackness. Hollis hesitated and held back. He grunted and grabbed her by her waist, pushing her violently into the room. Both of her knees slammed into the floor, and she cried out. But her cry was covered by the slamming of the door and the sliding of a metal bolt.

She screamed in frustration. The silence was complete, but she sensed rather than heard she was not alone.

"Is anyone else in here?"

Nothing.

She rose from a puddle of water. Except for the sliver of light coming from the bottom of the door, the room was in darkness. She rubbed her bruised knees, held her arms straight out in front of her, and ventured cautiously toward the door. Once there, she began to walk along the wall as she had in the previous room. The room didn't seem to be as big, but she wanted to be sure. The activity helped her fight her feelings of fear and alarm. Those would do her no good. She made her way to the first corner and turned with the wall, skirting what felt like the long side. She went back and started counting her steps from the corner. Fifteen, say twelve feet long, if she allowed for the size of her feet. She started counting from the next corner: five…six….

A low moan.

An adrenaline rush triggered her rapid heartbeat.

"Hello? Where are you?"

Silence.

"Please," she begged. "Speak again."

Stillness.

She continued to walk along the wall: ten feet to the next corner. Swallowing hard, she envisioned a diagonal line and began walking across the middle of the room. There were several more puddles, and her feet squished water inside her flats.

"I know I'm not alone. We're clearly locked in here together." She kept her voice low and steady, holding tight on the scream that wanted to escape her lips. Reaching the corner, she walked along the wall to the next corner to make a diagonal across the room.

She'd only taken three steps when she stumbled over a bundle of what felt like clothes, and the plaintive cry that emerged caused her to fall back on her bottom.

"Who are you?"

No answer.

She crawled toward the shadowed head of a figure curled in the fetal position.

She tentatively reached out and brushed back hair from the face. Like a blind person, she lightly felt the features with her fingertips. Sticky liquid covered them as she sat back on her heels. Silent tears slipped down her cheeks.

Vince.

SHE FUMBLED FOR his wrist. His pulse was very faint, but it was there. He moaned when she put her hand down on his side. She felt more blood, and there was something wrong with the angle of his leg. She bit her bottom lip in dismay. At least he was unconscious. She sat back on her heels, taking deep breaths to bring her thoughts into sharp focus.

They would be out looking for her. They'd go to Justin's apartment first, and then…and then, unless someone had seen the van, the search would end there. How long had she been here? It could already be tomorrow. Was it possible Vince still had one of his phones? Maybe the signal had barely gotten through before they lost his location or the battery died. Cook was still looking for him.

She gently lifted the flap on his pants leg pocket. His scream cut her to the heart.

"Vince, I'm so sorry," she cried out. "I didn't know how badly you were hurt."

He blinked several times, lifted then slowly shook his head. He stared in her direction.

"Hollis?" he whispered.

"It's me." She smiled, and then frowned. "We've been worried sick about you."

"Do you have any water?" he rasped.

"No, but wait." She dipped the edge of her jacket into a puddle and sniffed it, and then she licked it. Ugh. Who knew what bacteria it contained? But Vince was clearly dehydrated.

She went quickly through her pants pockets, but other than a pen, some business cards, and a small cellophane bag of peanuts, she was at a loss. She looked around the darkened space, and her lips formed a thin, grim line. She carefully dumped the peanuts in her pocket and used the cellophane bag as a scoop. She half dipped, half pulled the wrinkled bag into a nearby puddle and could feel rather than see the few tablespoons of water inside.

She dribbled the water into his mouth. He lapped it up. She repeated the motion twice more before he spoke again.

"How long?"

"You've been gone two days. I think this is Sunday."

She was already scooping up more water. She could barely see his features in the dark, but he drew her hand to his mouth. He ran his tongue over his lips.

"Thank you," he murmured. "It tastes like metal, but it's champagne to me."

"Vince, we're going to get out of here. I think they left us to die—that's the good news." She stood and started tapping the walls.

He lay his head down with a moan. His raspy voice came out of the dark. "If that's the good news, what… what's the bad news?"

She bent over him. "What did they do to hurt you?"

"My leg…it's broken bad. My right eye is messed up and…and they gave me heroin."

Hollis winced. "You're shivering." She took off her jacket and placed it over his shoulders.

"I think... I think they thought an overdose would kill me, but it helped me get through the pain." He chuckled weakly.

"You want to know what the good news is?" Her chest swelled with anger, and she stood and started to circle the room. "The good news is the man who held me didn't let me see his face, or even hear his voice." She looked at the faint shape on the floor. "That's the good news, because they don't want to kill us. But I know who he is, and we're going to be rescued."

Vince said nothing.

"The main warehouse floor was dry when I came through," she said. "But this concrete floor has puddles. Where does the water come from?" She knew she was talking mostly to herself. She hoped that Vince had slipped back into unconsciousness. His pain had to be indescribable.

"Maybe...maybe a window?" His voice faltered.

"Yes, a window, or a door." She walked along the wall, feeling with her hands. "I wish I knew where we are."

Vince coughed. "Down from...from Emeryville. You know that...little stretch of the estuary that runs into... University Avenue?" He coughed again.

Hollis could tell the efforts he was making were draining him.

"Yes," she said with excitement. "It runs along Highway 80. There's a group of small industrial offices, warehouses, and old buildings." She returned to tapping the wall. "How did you figure it out?"

"I used to do...do drugs here."

It was her turn to be silent, as she once more deliberately and slowly felt her way along the wall. She came to a deep puddle and bent down to bring more of the nasty liquid to his open mouth.

"I'll return with help," she whispered in his ear.

Hollis went back to feeling along the wall where the puddle was deepest. She stopped. There was some kind of cabinet, a small door lacking a knob or a lock. Using her fingernails, she ran them along the edge, trying to pry it open. It didn't budge.

"Vince, we are not going to die here," she said into silence.

Her next move broke her fingernail to the nail bed, making it too tender to use. The door was painted shut. Tears filled her eyes, but she began to pull with her other hand.

She didn't know when a small gap appeared, but ignoring the pain, she grabbed with the fingers of both hands and yanked as hard as she could. Many minutes later the door creaked open a little, then a lot. She was staring at empty shallow shelves, and at the top, a vent with a screen to the outside.

She looked into the darkened room. There was no sound from Vince.

Turning back to the cabinet, she stared up at the vent. She couldn't feel any direct air flowing, but the weather had been calm. It was going to be a squeeze. She didn't know what was on the other side of that screen, and to the extent she could see, how to escape. Because she did know one thing—their abductors would be back.

The wooden shelves were splintered and damp. She stepped onto the first one and it held, but when she settled her foot on the second shelf, it split in two. She cried out as a nail went through the bottom of her shoe; the darkness of the main room sucked up the sound. She fell back to the floor. Her tears were few and quiet.

There was no sound from Vince.

She needed the third shelf to hold if she were to get to the top. The fourth shelf would have to be removed; it was directly underneath the vent.

Back on her feet, she climbed onto the first shelf and then lifted her uninjured right foot as high as she could before setting it down on the third plank as close to the cabinet wall as possible. It creaked but held. Ducking her head and using her fist, she punched as hard as she could the center of the fourth shelf. Fortunately rain and moisture had done the most damage here, and the plank broke easily. She tossed the pieces to the floor.

She eased her left foot onto the far edge of the third shelf, and ignoring the pain, hoisted herself gingerly upright. Aided by moonlight, she could see out the vent. They were next to a high, grassy mound that sloped into the chilly waters of the estuary. Beyond that, Highway 80 and the San Francisco Bay were backlit by a full moon against a clear dark sky. She realized that by giving Vince her jacket she had only a thin blouse to protect her elbows as they rammed against the rusted vent screen. Her blouse tore, but the screen fell easily to the ground.

Hollis had overestimated the width of the opening, however, and only one shoulder could get through at a time. She had no leverage to get her legs through. Balancing on the tenuous strength of the shelf, she clenched her jaw in determination. She put her head out the hole, hoping to see runners or....

A crew team was making its way down the waterway. She frantically reached into her pants pocket and pulled out her business cards. She threw most of them out the vent window, screaming for help as they fluttered to the ground, just as gulls flew overhead, squawking loudly and drowning out her cries.

The canoe glided past.

She carefully stepped back down into the room. She didn't dare depend on the integrity of the shelf. She would have to try the vent again.

Darkness enveloped her, and it took a long moment for her eyes to adjust. Vince had not moved. If he did not get help soon, he would die.

Hollis knelt next to him. Her head throbbed and her foot hurt. She felt the dampness of her own blood along her arm. A thought flashed into her mind. Why hadn't her captor or captors questioned her? They had kidnapped her and brought her here, but what did they want? They probably thought Vince was dead. Did they plan for her to die the same way? Were they coming back to give her an overdose?

She had to make it easier for help to find them.

Evaluating the cabinet opening, she went over to the makeshift steps once more and made her way up to the vent. The air was turning cool. This time she put her arm through first and then her shoulder. In a short while, her waist was out, and that's when she saw two male runners making their way toward her.

"Help!"

Over and over, she cried out, "Help, please!"

Just as they came abreast of her location, one nudged the other, and they stopped and listened. They looked around but didn't see her. She waved unsteadily with both hands as she balanced on her stomach over the sill.

"Help!" she called out. "Please, over here."

Finally, one pointed and waved at her, and the other pulled out his phone.

"We see you," he yelled.

They ran to a nearby foot bridge, heading in her direction.

THIRTY-THREE

HOLLIS WOKE TO the muffled whirring of monitoring electronics. She blinked several times at the daylight slipping through the window blinds, and then turned her head. She was in a hospital. She closed her eyes.

When she opened them again, the light had faded and a nurse was checking her vitals.

"Well, hello," the nurse said cheerily. "I'm Nurse Leahy. We hoped to see your smile today."

"I'm in a hospital?" Hollis wrinkled her brow. "I remember the ambulance, but I don't remember passing out."

"That's because the doctor ordered a sedative. You're a little banged up."

She looked down at her bandaged arms and felt the wrapping around her head, chest, and foot. "I... I was trying to get through a vent. Is that how I got these?"

A voice came from the doorway. "You better believe it," John said, stepping over to her side. He bent over and kissed her on her forehead.

"Ah, your visitor. Although we're moving him out of the visitor category into the resident column. He's been here all along," the nurse chided over her shoulder as she left them alone.

John placed his hand in hers. "How do you feel?"

"Seeing you, I feel fine." She squeezed his hand, but the effort brought a wince. "Well, maybe just a little groggy, and sore, and I have a feeling I've been pumped with pain suppressants."

"Been there," he said. "They brought you here last night. But Vince—"

"Vince!" she called out. "How is he?" She tried to sit up but was stopped by a sharp pain. She lay back down. "Where is he?"

John put a firm hand on her shoulder on the only spot that wasn't wrapped. "He's alive. He was helicoptered to UC Med Center. Cook told me he was in pretty bad shape, but they expect him to recover."

She searched his face. "What is it you're not telling me?"

He sat in the chair next to her bed. "They don't know about his leg." He squeezed her hand. "It was pretty badly broken, and infection had set in. They're not sure they can save it."

Hollis gave a low moan. "How soon can I leave here?"

"The doctor is supposed to see you this afternoon. He'll likely release you then."

"I'm not going to wait." She threw back her covers, and a grimace of pain crossed her face. "I'm going to get dressed, and I'll check myself out if I have to. They can't make me stay. But first, I need to see Cook; I think I know who did it."

John shook his head. "Whoa, wait a minute. First, you don't have any clothes; the ones you had on were a filthy mess. Second, I brought a clean set of clothing, which I'm not giving up until the doctor releases you. Third, last night Cook was there at the warehouse. You don't remember? He's waiting to talk to you; he'll be here in a short while."

Her movement had triggered a monitor that emitted a low tone. Nurse Leahy appeared, turning off the machine. John retreated to a corner.

"Going somewhere?" she said as she checked the IV lines.

Hollis gripped the edge of the bed to steady her swimming head. "I need to go home. These are just cuts and bruises. I'd like to leave after I talk to the police. Can you ask the doctor to hurry?"

"Ms. Morgan, I'll see what I can do," Leahy said, "but the doctor won't keep you here any longer than necessary."

"Can you disconnect me from these tubes, so I can put my clothes on?"

The nurse cast a pleading look at John, who came over and sat on the side of the bed.

"Babe, I know you're worried about Vince, and I know you want to get the bad guys who did this," he said. "But this lady has to do her job and keep you quiet until the doc comes. I'll contact Cook and get him to send someone over in advance to get a statement. By that time, the doctor will be here, and we can all go home."

"Go call Cook," she said, lying back on her pillow. "Tell him to get someone here fast."

COOK MUST HAVE been waiting for the phone to ring. Barbara Kagan was there in twenty minutes. She stood over Hollis's bed.

"We've taken someone into custody, but he's not the killer. His prints were on top of yours in Eastland's apartment." She sighed. "Unfortunately, he's more afraid of the people who hired him than he is of us."

"Who is he? What does he look like?" Hollis asked.

"His name is Steve Munro. He's average height and weight, brown eyes and hair, kind of hyper," Kagan read from her notes. "He's got a sheet full of burglary and petty theft charges. He was released out of Chino about a year ago, and that's where he'll be going back, only for a lot longer."

"That sounds like the guy who kidnapped me." Hollis grimaced. "He spoke with a man named Phillip Carson to verify my identity. It was Carson who held me and Vince in that warehouse."

Kagan pulled up a chair and took out her notebook. "I'm going to be taking your story now, but you're still going to have to give and sign a formal statement." She paused. "Ah… Detective Cook said to tell you to let us take over. It's our job to get the bad guys."

"Then do your job." Hollis's temper flared. "There's an innocent kid who paid the price for your department's—"

"Hollis," John interjected. "Hold off."

He faced Kagan. "Detective, maybe you can take her story quickly, so we can leave as soon as the doctor gets here. We want to go to San Francisco to see Vince Colton."

Kagan held up her hand and nodded to Hollis. "I know you must be upset. I checked on Mr. Colton before I came here. He's in surgery, and they expect it to go on for a few hours."

"All right." Hollis's head pressed deeper into her pillow. "Let's get this over with."

It was many minutes before Hollis finished answering Kagan's questions. The detective was concise and pushed her to remember as many details as she could.

Hollis complied and was ready to say more when Cook came into the room.

He shook John's hand and gave an acknowledging nod to Hollis.

"Munro lawyered up," Cook said without preamble, "but not before he gave us collaborating information that will help us round up a few more members. He claims he only had one direct contact. Unfortunately, he didn't know his name, and he never saw the full team. His attorney is working on a deal with the DA."

"I think I can give you a name," Hollis said.

Cook peered at Hollis. "You said you think you know the killer. Who is he?"

"I said, 'I think,' but I know," Hollis pushed back. "I spoke with a guy who knew Justin Eastland in high school. They roomed together for a while. Both dated, if you can call it that, Marguerite Fields, and then went their separate ways. His name is Phil Carson. One thing stuck in my mind about him from our meeting: he had running shoes with bright red soles. I saw those same soles yesterday."

Cook and Kagan exchanged looks, and Kagan went out into the hallway, already speaking into the phone.

"There's one other thing, Cook," Hollis said, her voice gaining strength. "I also think I know what the killers were after, and where it is."

Cook had been about to follow Kagan out of the room, but he turned around and peered down at Hollis. "Please, Ms. Morgan, enlighten me."

"Justin was always reluctant to tell me what he found in that Nike bag. But, he did mention a data stick. His story had so many versions, it was hard to tell what was true and what wasn't at that point. But that Munro guy referred to a data disk. So that's the 'what.'" Hollis reached for the paper cup of water. "Then, just before Justin died, Vince said he thought he mumbled the word 'mug,' or 'rug.' When I was in Justin's apartment—before Munro found me—I found a rug that had been cut into along the fringe to form a pocket just big enough to hold a disk." She shifted onto her side. "Remember, Detective, that picture you had of Justin's apartment? It had three fringed rugs on the floor, but there was only one when I was there. I think Carson or Munro knew to look for a pocket in the rug, but didn't find the flash drive. Where are the other rugs?"

Cook rubbed his forehead. "They should be in the evidence room." He pulled out his phone. "Barbara, meet me in the evidence room in about thirty minutes. I'll explain." He paused. It was clear she was still talking. "Good work. I'll be right there." He clicked off.

Hollis and John gave him a curious look.

"I've got to get back to the department. They just arrested Carson. Evidently, he's ready to roll over on his colleagues. He doesn't realize we have them without his testimony. He'll do time for murder and kidnapping." Slipping the phone into his jacket breast pocket, he looked at her with respect. "They told me this is your first criminal case. You're good at it. Thank you for helping us out."

Hollis smiled with pleasure. "You're very welcome."

He nodded at John and left.

John bent over her. "You know how you told me you felt when you thought I was dead. Now I understand." He gently touched her cheek. "This may not be the best time in the world to say this, but I have your full attention. I'm so proud of you—you are an amazing woman.

I can't imagine living a happy life without you, Hollis." He wrinkled his brow. "I can't imagine my years ahead without you in them, without worrying about you, without thinking about you, without sharing with you all that I am." He held her hand. "You make mè crazy, Hollis Morgan, but I love only you. I know we talked about a future before, but I'm tired of talking. Will you marry me—soon?"

Hollis didn't realize she'd been holding her breath until she laughed and said, "Yes."

EPILOGUE

FIFTY BELOVED WEDDING guests waited expectantly in the small chapel nestled in the Berkeley Hills. The air was redolent with the scent of flowers. White roses, baby's breath, and Asiatic lilies decorated the altar and the ends of the pews.

Hollis looked down on the gathering from behind a column in the organ loft.

Stephanie stood at the altar, wearing a sophisticated azure-blue suit that set off her eyes and complemented her figure. She glowed with happiness. Opposite her and next to John was Dan, a very handsome best man with eyes only for the maid of honor.

Vince sat at the far side of the pew in the first row. His leg, in a thigh-high cast thrust out into the aisle, needed one more surgery. He would always walk with a limp, but he would walk. Katie sat next to him taking pictures with a point-and-shoot camera, ignoring the glare of the professional photographer who clearly resented the amateur competition.

Next to them were Rena and Mark. In her fifth month of pregnancy, Rena was starting to show. Mark kept a protective arm around her shoulders, and they both beamed with pride.

Behind them sat Penny and Gordon. Penny looked stern, trying not to cry, and Gordon was sneaking glances around the chapel, probably scoping out potential clients. He'd promised to leave his phone in his car. Doubtful.

The rest of Triple D filled the next two pews. Ed Simmons was there, furtively looking at his watch. Eleanor nudged him with a frown.

On the other side sat the rest of the Fallen Angels. Gene was there with his partner, and Miller arrived with his young daughter. Much to the members' surprise, Richard came with his wife. According to Rena, who gave Hollis early reports on the guests, Denise Kleh seemed like a very nice woman.

"I'm not kidding, Hollis," Rena insisted. "I had a chance to speak with her for a little while. She's nothing like Richard. He made her sound pretentious, but she's not. She's very down to earth."

"Go figure," they said in unison and laughed.

In front of the Fallen Angels sat her family. Her mother clung to her father as if afraid he was going to leave her to interact with strangers on her own. But to her credit, she sat tall and her face did not wear its usual pained expression. Dad looked pleased, as did her sister Rita and the girls. There was a moment when Hollis wanted her father to walk her down the aisle, but if it meant keeping peace with her mother, she would gladly walk alone.

Joe somehow felt her eyes on them and turned to gaze over his shoulder at her. Her brother was so handsome in his uniform. They exchanged smiles.

It was time to get started.

The ceremony went by too fast and in triple slow motion at the same time. She couldn't stop smiling, and John had a boyish grin that didn't go away. Their eyes never left each other's. They recited vows they'd written themselves, simple and heartfelt, and their responses were filled with the resolve that comes from reaching the finish line. She could hear a few guests sniffling.

Finally, John reached for her hand and slid a gold band on her finger, and she did the same with his.

They both wore wide grins. Their guests chuckled.

The minister raised his voice, "And now, it's my pleasure to introduce Mr. and Mrs. John Faber."

* * * * *

R. FRANKLIN JAMES grew up in the San Francisco Bay Area and graduated from the University of California at Berkeley. As a UC Berkeley grad, she cultivated a different type of writing—legislation and public policy. After a career of public advocacy and serving as Deputy Mayor for the City of Los Angeles, she went back to her first love—writing. In 2013, her debut novel, *The Fallen Angels Book Club*, was published by Camel Press. Her second book in the Hollis Morgan Mystery Series, *Sticks & Stones*, was released in 2014, and her third book, *The Return of the Fallen Angels Book Club*, was released in 2015, followed by *The Trade List* in 2016 and in 2017, *The Bell Tolls*.

R. Franklin James lives in Northern California with her husband.

For more information, go to www.rfranklinjames.com.